SPY GODDESS

Live and Let Shop

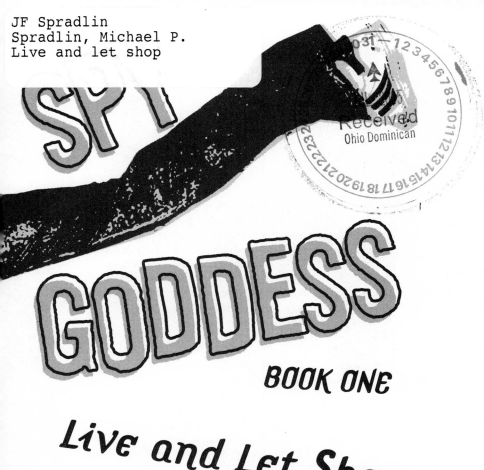

SPY GODDESS

BOOK ONE

Live and Let Shop

MICHAEL P. SPRADLIN

HarperCollins*Publishers*

Spy Goddess: Live and Let Shop
Copyright © 2005 by Michael P. Spradlin
All rights reserved. No part of this book may be used or reproduced
in any manner whatsoever without written permission except in the
case of brief quotations embodied in critical articles and reviews.
Printed in the United States of America. For information address
HarperCollins Children's Books, a division of HarperCollins
Publishers, 1350 Avenue of the Americas, New York, NY 10019.
www.harperchildrens.com

Library of Congress Cataloging-in-Publication Data
Spradlin, Michael P.
    Live and let shop / Michael P. Spradlin.— 1st ed.
        p.   cm. — (Spy goddess ; bk. 1)
    Summary: Beverly Hills teenager Rachel Buchanan gets in trouble
with the law and winds up at mysterious Blackthorn Academy in
Pennsylvania, where she uncovers secrets about the school and
becomes entangled in a case of international espionage.
    ISBN 0-06-059407-1 — ISBN 0-06-059408-X (lib. bdg.)
    [1. Boarding Schools—Fiction. 2. Schools—Fiction. 3. Juvenile
delinquency—Fiction. 4. Spies—Fiction. 5. Supernatural—Fiction.]
I. Title.
PZ7.S7645Li 2005   2004008851
[Fic]—dc22   CIP
                                                            AC

Typography by R. Hult
1 2 3 4 5 6 7 8 9 10

First Edition

This book is for my daughter,

Rachel Leigh Spradlin,

the toughest girl I know.

—MS

TABLE OF CONTENTS

SPY GODDESS

Live and Let Shop

PART ONE

CHAPTER ONE

The End of My Life as I Know It

The cop car I rode in the night I got arrested was really clean. Spotless, almost. So was the station house. It wasn't like the police stations you see on TV, where there are druggies and lowlifes everywhere you look and everything is total chaos. It was pretty quiet, very neat, and there didn't seem to be much going on. It reminded me of the locker room at Dad's country club. I guess there's not a lot of serious crime in Beverly Hills. Except for me, of course—Rachel Buchanan, one-girl crime wave.

We only got caught that night because Boozer made an illegal left turn in the car he'd boosted. Unluckily for us, a cop happened to drive by at exactly the wrong moment. So much of life is just timing.

Boozer is so smooth, he probably could have talked his way out of it, but instead he panicked and took off. So there we were in a high-speed chase. The weird thing was, I thought it was funny. For some reason, when I get scared or nervous—or apparently in a high-speed chase—I start to laugh. Maybe I'm a psycho. I'll get on a roller coaster at Magic Mountain with a drop straight down, and while everyone is screaming at the top of their lungs, I'm sitting there laughing like an idiot. It's this really weird nervous laugh that I can't stop. I wonder what a shrink would say about that?

Anyway, so Boozer, Jamie, and Grego were scared and screaming the whole time the cop was chasing us, and when Boozer ran the car up onto a lawn, they piled out right away and took off running. I was laughing so hard in the backseat that I couldn't move, and that's how I got busted.

The cop ordered me out of the car and asked me what I thought was so funny. Stealing a car and driving it up on some-body's lawn? And who were my friends and where did they go? And I was in a lot of trouble, missy, make no mistake about it. And blah, blah, blah, blah, blah. I couldn't stop laughing, so he hustled me into his car and off we went to the station.

I wound up sitting on a bench outside the interview room, where a detective named Daniels asked me all kinds of questions about who took the car. He kept saying I'd better tell them what they wanted to know or I'd be in worse trouble. I told him to stuff it because there's no way I was telling the cops who I was with. So he called my parents and invited them down to spend a little quality time with me at the Beverly Hills PD.

It took about an hour for Dad to show up—of course, with the ever-present cell phone glued to his ear. Probably calling Marvin. Marvin is his attorney. Check that. Marvin is more than Dad's attorney. He's like Dad's most favorite person ever. Dad looks at Marvin and sees dollar signs. He just loves Marvin, who is quite possibly the most boring human being on the face of the earth.

No sign of Mom. Probably at home with her coffee cup full of "medicine." I bet she was already working the phones in the neighborhood, trying to find out if word had spread about her daughter the criminal, and wondering how she was going to keep this out of the *Beverly Hills Gazette*.

"Hi, Charles! Always nice to see you," I said. "Mom busy?"

He didn't even stop to ask if I was okay. He skipped right to the yelling part.

"What were you thinking stealing a car!" he said.

"I didn't steal anything. I—" As usual he didn't let me finish.

"Do you have any idea what kind of trouble you're in? Do you realize what you've put us through?" By "us" I wasn't sure if he meant him and Mom or him and Marvin. Any time he spent having to deal with me meant less opportunity to make even more zillions of dollars.

"What do you have to say for yourself?" he said.

"I didn't do anything," I said. "I was just out with some friends."

"You mean that bunch of juvenile delinquents?"

"Ouch, Dad. I mean, really, that hurts."

"You think this is funny?" He was getting angrier.

"Well, this part not so much. The high-speed chase had its moments, though."

"You think you've got it all figured out, don't you?" he said. "This isn't the first little scrape you've been in. Shoplifting, vandalism, and now you've graduated to Grand Theft Auto. That's a felony! You realize you'll have to appear before a juvenile court judge again?"

"Juvenile court! Again? That'll be great," I said. "Maybe you and Mom can both make it this time. We'll pack a lunch and make a day of it!"

"Keep cracking wise, Rachel. You seem to think it's all a great big joke. Well, if you won't cooperate with the police, that's your problem. No Marvin, no other attorneys, no help from us. You're on your own."

CHAPTER TWO

How I Got Here

The next couple of weeks seemed surprisingly normal. Sure, for the first couple of days Charles and Cynthia were really upset with me. There was a lot of yelling and the using of first names. Whenever they are mad at each other, or me, they use their first names a lot. "Charles this" and "Cynthia that" and "Charles, *do* something." But after that, as usual, they sort of forgot about me again. Charles even cooled off to the degree that he said he'd actually send Marvin to court with me this time instead of one of Marvin's junior associates. But as far as he was concerned, whatever the judge decided was too good for me. I was grounded, of course, so I stayed in my room, surfing the Web and watching TV when I wasn't in school.

The day after I was unjustly incarcerated, I got to school to find Boozer, Jamie, and Grego all waiting for me by my locker. They were kind of hovering and pacing back and forth. It put a lump in my throat that they were so worried about me. That went away pretty fast, though.

"Did you tell?" That was the first thing out of Boozer's mouth. Not "Are you okay?" or "Are you in trouble?" or "Did they work you over with a rubber hose?"

"Of course not," I said. "I didn't tell them anything."

Boozer and Grego let out visible sighs of relief. They had both been in a lot more trouble than me before, and if I ratted them out, they'd really be in for it.

"I don't understand why you didn't run," Grego said. "You wouldn't be in this mess if you'd taken off like the rest of us."

"I don't know. I just froze, I guess. Anyway, I have to go to court in a couple of weeks—" I started, but Boozer interrupted me.

"Yeah, well, your dad's rich, so your lawyer will get you off. Don't worry about it. Come on, guys," Boozer said. They all followed Boozer down the hall and left me standing by my locker alone.

That got me thinking. I'm not the kind of person who does that very often—think about things, I mean. Mostly I just try to get through the day. But for some reason, being at the cop house stayed on my mind. I kept wondering, *How did I get to this point?* What was I thinking going along with my friends, the ones who took off at the first sign of trouble and left me footing the bill for a stolen car? Truth be told, I really didn't know the answer.

Maybe it all started when Grandpa died, a couple of years

ago. It kind of sounds like a cop-out, I know. But I remember being a lot happier when Gramps was still around. I think he was the only person in the world who loved me unconditionally. He was the coolest, always spoiling me and making me feel like I was important to him. I mean, I guess Charles and Cynthia loved me. Maybe. So long as I didn't cause them any grief and spoke only when spoken to. Then Gramps died and left Buchanan Enterprises to Charles, and everything changed. Charles was obsessed with removing all evidence that Gramps had ever built the company in the first place. He wanted it to be bigger and better and to make more money than Grandpa ever did, and Grandpa had already made hundreds of millions. So he spent all of his time at work, and, of course, Cynthia hated that so she started taking it out on me. Because obviously it had to be my fault.

Up until then, I'd been pretty much a normal kid. I did okay in school and made decent grades. Then Cynthia started spending all of her time at the gym and with the ladies from her club, and when she was around the house, which wasn't often, the coffee cup of "medicine" was never very far out of reach. Charles was always at the office or away on business, so that left me pretty much alone.

So for the last two years, from age thirteen on, I pretty much raised myself. And I started not caring what Charles and Cynthia thought about where I was and what I did. I started to cut class—not a lot, but enough. (They have truant officers even in Beverly Hills, after all.) And I stopped caring very much about school when I was there. For all I know, maybe it wasn't

Gramps dying at all—maybe it was hormones, or maybe it was just boredom. Soon I started hanging out with Boozer and his gang.

Boozer was a couple of years older than me, and I have to admit I was kind of flattered that he noticed me. I mean, me with a bad boy! It's no secret how he got the nickname Boozer, and he's what Charles would call part of the "bad element." Just what I was looking for.

We went out a few times, and I got to be friends with Jamie and Grego. At least, I thought we were friends, until they ditched me after the car chase. I mean, I know they've all been in a lot worse trouble then me, so I can understand that they couldn't let themselves get caught. But they still left me there.

Boozer kept his distance for the two weeks before my court date. After that day at school he really didn't talk to me at all, and I guess I couldn't complain, because it wasn't like we were a serious couple or anything. I thought I had made it clear that I wouldn't turn him in and I guess he was grateful, but he sure had a funny way of showing it. Jamie and Grego stayed away too, like I had the stink of trouble on me and they weren't going to get close enough for it to rub off on them.

So I had a lot of time to think about what I was going to do when I got to court. I went on the Internet to look up stuff about juvenile delinquents and joyriding. One of the things I read was an *L.A. Times* article about the Juvenile Detention Center in Los Angeles. The reporter interviewed a fifteen-year-old girl who had been sent there for drug possession. It was not a pretty picture: gangs, fights, knives, and bad stuff going down. Great. Just the place for a Beverly Hills Princess.

According to the Juvenile Code on the California Legal Aid website, joyriding was a Class D felony. But Marvin said that I was going to be charged with Grand Theft Auto, and that was a lot more serious. That meant jail time. I had to think of a way out of this. I watched a lot of reruns of *The Practice* on Court TV to look for tips or loopholes in the law.

Two weeks to the day after we "borrowed" the car, I was off to the Juvenile Court Building for my hearing. Charles had to go to San Diego for a meeting on some big condo deal, and Cynthia "couldn't handle the stress." So it was just old Marv and me. Great. Marvin was older than my dad. He was bald and chubby with a really awful comb-over that he thought made him look younger but only made him look balder.

The judge was a woman about my mom's age, which is late thirties. Her nameplate said "Judge Kerrigan." She had dark hair, done up in a bun so she looked really severe, and she wore these huge geeky glasses that she perched on the end of her nose. She was looking at a file folder that I guessed must have been my life story. Snore.

Marvin did a lot of talking. And I think that this is where things started to go wrong. See, Marvin has this *really* monotone voice that just drones on and on. He comes to dinner at our house a lot, and whenever he starts talking in that voice, it's all I can do to keep from slamming my eyelids shut and falling into a coma. And now the same thing was happening here.

I felt pretty sure that Marvin would keep me out of jail.

Despite all the stuff on the Internet about the law, Marvin is a big-time lawyer and I felt pretty safe. I mean, people like me don't go to jail. And since he was so boring and his voice made me sleepy, I didn't really think I had to pay much attention to what was going on. So instead I watched the judge and silently made fun of her hairstyle. *Sure, judge, that style is all the rage . . . if it was 1957!* Hah. That was a good one. *"Our next model is Judge Kerrigan, and famed stylist Bobby Brown has given her a look she calls 'Jail Matron.'"* That was pretty funny too. I was actually starting to enjoy myself a little.

But I didn't count on Judge "Soon to be the bane of my existence" Kerrigan. I guess I missed her asking me a question, because the next thing I know she's speaking to me in a really loud voice.

"Are we *boring* you, Ms. Buchanan?" She peered down from the bench.

"No," I said, snapping back from my daydream.

"No, Your Honor. That is how you address the bench."

"No, Your Honor." Then I muttered "whatever" under my breath.

"You think you're being clever?" she said. Oops. I didn't think she'd hear me. Now she was really boring into me with those eyes. It was starting to make me nervous, and I had a little tingling feeling in my stomach that maybe this wasn't going to work out the way I hoped. Stuff from that article about the Detention Center started rolling through my brain. Like about the food being really bad there.

"Let's see," the judge said. "Grand Theft Auto, Evading a

Police Officer, Resisting Arrest, Malicious Destruction of Property, and Failure to Cooperate with a Police Investigation. That's quite a list. Do you have anything to say for yourself?"

Marvin started to talk, but the judge shushed him without taking her eyes off me.

"Well, for one thing, I wasn't really resisting arrest," I pointed out. "I was just laughing."

The judge chose to ignore that.

"I see from your file that you've been a regular high-achiever lately. You've already been given probation for shoplifting and suspended from school for cheating on an exam—"

"They couldn't prove that," I interrupted her.

"I am talking now. You listen. Got that?"

"Yes," I said. I was starting to feel worse. The article had also said that in the last six months, five different guards had been injured during fights among the inmates. Fights? I don't fight with anyone. Except Charles and Cynthia.

She looked at me again. "Yes?" she said.

"Yes, Your Honor."

"Aha. So you can learn. Perhaps you're not as stupid as you've been acting lately."

I thought it best not to thank her for the compliment. Was that a compliment?

Marvin took this opportunity to open his pie hole.

"Your Honor—" he started to say.

"Not interested, Counselor."

Marvin got a really weird look on his face, like he'd been slapped, and then sat back down and started fussing with some papers on the table in front of us.

The judge closed the file and looked at me.

"Where are your parents?" she asked.

"Busy, I guess," I said. "As usual." She stared at me for ages before speaking again.

"I do not like what I'm seeing here. I've seen a thousand kids like you, Ms. Buchanan. You're unhappy and you don't know why. Maybe it's because you come from a rich family and you feel guilty about it. Maybe your parents ignore you. All I know for sure is you're on a fast track to Juvenile Detention. In fact, I don't think you're giving me a whole lot of choice here."

"Your Honor, my client—"

"Still not interested in your opinion, Counselor. I believe I have an obligation to the people to remove a problem from the community."

Now I was really feeling sick to my stomach. *Remove.* She'd said "remove." One of the kids at school knew someone who'd gone to Juvie. He said that you only got one phone call a week and if you broke any rules you'd get no visitors. I'd never survive that! I'm a people person! I need my visitors!

No one was saying anything, so Marvin started in again.

"Your Honor, Rachel's parents are sorry they couldn't be here today, but circumstances prevented it. They would like me to assure the court that they believe Rachel is basically a good kid. You know how teenagers can be, a little high-strung, and maybe things have gotten a little out of hand. But—"

Judge Interrupter struck again.

"Counselor, I've heard every excuse you can imagine.

Rachel has been on a downward spiral toward serious trouble for months, and obviously her parents haven't done anything about it." I would have enjoyed this if the judge hadn't been talking about me. I wished Charles and Cynthia had been there to hear it.

The judge turned back to me.

"I think a stint in Juvenile Detention might be the wake-up call you need."

She raised her gavel. "Thirty days—"

Marvin started to stand up and say something, but I beat him to it. I hadn't spent all that time in my room watching *Law & Order* reruns for nothing.

"I object!" I shouted.

Everyone went quiet and stared at me.

The judge peered down from the bench with one eyebrow cocked.

"*You* object?" she said.

I had also read that you only got to take showers every other day in Juvie. I'm a stickler for good personal hygiene.

"Yes, I object," I said. *Uh-oh. Better think of something quick.* In my head I ran through every courtroom and lawyer movie and TV show I could think of. What would that cute guy on *The Practice* do now?

"On what grounds?" the judge asked. The courtroom was completely quiet. The judge looked like she was waiting for my next move.

"I object because . . . because . . . you can't handle the truth!" Yeah, Tom Cruise and Jack Nicholson in *A Few Good Men*. That should work. I had just seen it on cable the week before.

The judge sort of smirked again.

"I've seen that movie too, Ms. Buchanan, but I'll humor you. What exactly is the truth that I can't handle?"

Dang it. Now I had to do more thinking. This was not a good day.

"The truth is this is a gross injustice. The punishment you're suggesting is way out of proportion to the alleged crime. Not to mention the fact that I'm clearly not receiving competent representation here. I mean, have you listened to his voice? It's a wonder the entire courtroom isn't asleep. Besides that, Marvin doesn't know anything about Juvenile law—not that he needs to know anything, because I didn't break any laws. Furthermore, as I'm sure you're aware, there is a constitutional amendment against cruel and unusual punishment, and sending me to the Juvenile Center would certainly qualify as such." And that was definitely the truth, because I'd read in the article that you were also denied Internet access, and if that isn't "cruel and unusual," I don't know what is. Might as well just shoot me in the head.

I held my breath. Marvin was giving me dirty looks, obviously upset with my crack about his lull-you-to-sleep voice.

"Are you quite finished?" the judge asked.

I couldn't think of anything else to say.

"All right. I'll make you a deal, Ms. Buchanan. If you'll tell me right now who was with you when the car was stolen, I'll reduce your charge from a felony to a misdemeanor.

Then you won't go to juvenile detention. The clock is ticking, Ms. Buchanan."

That's her idea of a deal?

I couldn't think clearly. She said *I* wasn't giving her a choice? This just wasn't an option for me.

"No," I said.

"Excuse me?" said the judge.

"I said no. I'm not telling you anything about who I was with that night. I didn't take the car and I didn't resist arrest or any of that other stuff you're trying to pin on me. But I'm not naming names. I won't sell out my friends just because you think you can boss me around." *There, that ought to teach her.*

"Rachel, perhaps—" Marvin started to speak. But I gave him my best glare and he shut up.

"Let me get this straight," the judge said. "Your so-called friends,"—and she made that little "air quote" marks motion when she said it; I hate it when people do that—"the ones who actually stole the car, drove the car onto a lawn, and then left you facing arrest . . . these are the people you're protecting?"

"That's right. I guess you'll just have to send me to Juvie. But friends are friends, and I'm not pointing the finger at them to save myself. You probably wouldn't understand that, since I doubt someone as mean as you has any friends. I don't think it'll do any good to send me to Juvie, but if you have to, I guess you have to send me."

I hoped the outfits in Juvie wouldn't clash too horribly with my complexion.

Marvin took a huge breath and threw his head in his hands, muttering, "Oh my God" under his breath.

For a moment I thought the judge almost smiled, but from what I'd seen of her personality so far, that seemed unlikely. And then she got an almost evil glint in her eye and I wondered if I'd pushed it too far with that crack about her not having any friends. She didn't say anything else for a really long time. She just sat there staring at me like she knew something about me but couldn't quite place it. Then she finally spoke.

"All right, Ms. Buchanan. Frankly, I think you're being stupid. I do admire loyalty, even misguided loyalty. However, you've committed a crime and I have an obligation to the people to protect their lives and property. And I won't even mention your deplorable behavior in my courtroom. So I can't simply let you off the hook, but there is an alternative option." She kept staring at me. It was giving me the creeps.

"Anything. I'll agree to anything." The plain truth of it is, I felt like I was inches away from being sent to the slammer, and the very thought terrified me. I don't like admitting to myself that I'm scared of anything, but right then I was more scared than I'd ever been.

The judge steepled her fingers.

Somehow I sensed a smart remark wouldn't be so smart.

"Your Honor," I remembered to add at the last minute.

"I'll be frank with you, Rachel," she said. First time she called me Rachel. I felt us growing closer. "I don't want to send you to Juvenile Detention. I think you'd survive it fine, but I don't think it would do any good." Me? Survive Juvie? Who was she kidding? I'd be dead in an hour.

"So this is the alternative." *Oh boy, here it comes,* I thought. I saw myself in one of those really tacky orange jumpsuits, picking up trash along the Santa Monica Freeway, part of a rebellious, yet quietly heroic, teenage chain gang.

"I'm listening," I said. She cocked her head and looked like she was about to come down on me again, so I hastily added "Your Honor." Dang, I kept forgetting that.

"I'm on the board of directors of a boarding school in eastern Pennsylvania, near Washington, D.C. It is a school for students of all ages and from a variety of backgrounds. Many come there for the excellent education. But many of them are like you, Ms. Buchanan: troubled, on the wrong side of the law. Some are orphans, some are unwanted by their parents, others are there for a variety of other reasons. The school helps turn them around.

"So this is my deal," she went on. "You will attend this school for a minimum of one year. Complete the year and you'll have all the charges dropped from your record. You'll be free to come home or stay at the school. It will be totally up to you. But leave the school before the year is up, get kicked out or in trouble in any way, and it's right back to California and the William G. Wilson Hall for Juvenile Delinquents."

I couldn't believe this! She wanted to send me to some weirdo school in Pennsyl-freakin'-vania? With a bunch of creeps and nutcases from all over the place? No way. Me and my big mouth. Why can't I ever just shut up? Instead of thirty days in the slammer, she now wanted to send me away for a whole *year*? What kind of idiot did she think I was? Juvie had to be better than this—or maybe not, but at least it was only a month, assuming I lived that long.

Plus, I'd have to leave Beverly Hills and all my friends. I am such a California person. Were there malls in Pennsylvania? I didn't think I could even *spell* Pennsylvania. I was about to say something, but Marvin beat me to the punch.

"Your Honor, this is highly irregular . . . the sentencing guidelines . . ."

It was becoming clear that Judge Kerrigan had little patience for ol' Marv—about the only thing we had in common.

"Counselor. I'm guessing you haven't been in a courtroom in twenty years." Hah! She had that right. As far as I could tell, Marvin pretty much stayed within three feet of Charles most of the time, and I'd had to give him directions to the courthouse on the way over here! "I'll bet you've never been in a juvenile court in your life. So I don't think you really want to debate the finer points of juvenile law with me, do you?"

Marvin got that *I've just been slapped* look on his face again, then took his cell phone off his belt and asked the judge if he could call my dad. She nodded.

I decided the only thing that would work now was out-and-out defiance.

"I'm not going to some lame school in Pennsylvania. I'll do my time in Juvie instead."

"She'll go." Marvin, taking a stand at last. Except—what?

"What!" I said.

20

"You heard me. I've just spoken to your father. He thinks it's an excellent idea, and tells me to instruct you to stop arguing with the judge and make the arrangements."

"I'm not going."

Marvin shrugged and held out the cell phone like he was daring me to hear it for myself.

This day just kept getting worse. I had figured we'd breeze in, let Marvin schmooze the judge, get a few extra months tacked onto the probation, and be home before lunch. Now I had to make Sophie's Choice. How much does that suck?

I looked at the judge, and there was definitely a trace of a self-satisfied smile on her face. I'd been had. I opened my mouth, but no words came out.

"Listen, Rachel," she said. "I know that this school can help. It will change you. For the better. You might even find whatever it is you feel is missing in your life, that is causing you to act like such an idiot."

I resented that. "I'm not an idiot," I protested.

"I didn't say you were an idiot. I said you were acting like one."

Oh, that judge.

"So. What's it going to be, Rachel? Jail or a second chance?"

I felt totally alone. No parents. No friends. Marvin was useless.

"Okay. I'll go. I'll go to the stupid school." From everything I'd read and heard, Juvie was not a fit for Rachel Buchanan. Besides, a nugget of a plan was starting to form in my head. Maybe I could get out of this somehow, but not if I was in the slammer. It would have to be easier to escape this mess from a boarding school than a prison. Even if the school was in Pennsyl-freakin'-vania.

Still, it felt like an eight-hundred-pound gorilla was sitting on my chest.

"Excellent," the judge said. She looked at Marvin. "Counselor, let's begin the paperwork. Rachel will have one week to say good-bye to her friends and travel to Pennsylvania. She will report to Mr. Jonathon Kim, the headmaster of the school. He will compile and send quarterly reports on her progress and behavior to this court and her parents." She dismissed Marvin with a wave.

We stood up from our chairs and started toward the door of the courtroom. Marvin put his hand out as if to shepherd me to the door. I turned back to the judge.

"Your Honor, can I ask you a question?"

"Of course," she said.

"How do you know this is such a great deal for me? You said you were on the board of this school. But what is that, a couple of meetings a couple times a year? You seem so sure it can turn my life around. But how do you know? What is so special about this particular school?"

This time the judge actually smiled. Clearly, for at least three-tenths of a second, her lips moved in an upward direction. And I think she even made a chuckling sound. But I wasn't sure, because it could easily have been a witch's cackle. Or the death rattle of some primitive beast that lived in a cave and came out only at night to feast on human flesh.

She opened her desk drawer, pulled out a brochure, and handed it to me. On the cover of the brochure were the words "Blackthorn Academy" in large white type, plus a picture of what looked like a giant wedge of stainless-steel cheese cut into the side of a mountain and surrounded by about five million trees.

The judge got a really mysterious look on her face.

"You'll find out soon enough," she said.

CHAPTER THREE

Welcome to Blackthorn Academy

So in seven short days I was gone from Beverly Hills and all of my friends. I couldn't believe how fast it happened.

I don't really remember much about leaving the courtroom or the ride home. That night I called Jamie, and she couldn't believe it when I told her. The next day at school, word had spread like wildfire. Rachel Buchanan, of the Beverly Hills Buchanans, was being sent up the river. Even if the river was really a "special school."

When Boozer heard the news, he said he was sorry, which was cool, and that he wanted to throw me a big going-away bash, which was sweet, except that knowing Boozer, the going-away bash would probably involve large crowds, numerous illegal substances, and quite possibly the Los Angeles Lakers cheerleaders.

That would be all I needed, to get busted at a rave right before leaving for my jail sentence . . . I mean, my jail/school sentence.

It seemed as if I spent the week walking through gauze or looking at myself in a fun-house mirror that wasn't quite reflecting right. By the end of the week, I was freaking out. I didn't want to go. Even though Charles and Cynthia were no great shakes as parents, this was still home. It was a place to sleep and food to eat and clean clothes whenever the maid did the laundry. I briefly thought about running away. But Charles would just hire a million private eyes to track me down and I'd end up in Juvie anyway.

Marvin drove me to the airport. Cynthia stayed home because she didn't think she could handle it (big surprise), and God knows you'd never want to make a scene in public. Charles, of course, had to be out of town for a "deal." In any case, Judge Kerrigan had made it painfully clear to Marvin that she was holding him personally responsible for me getting on that plane. And if she found out I didn't get on it, there would be "hell to pay." Marvin fell all over himself assuring the judge that he'd take care of it.

So Marvin got me on the plane and wished me well and that was that. Good-bye, Beverly Hills.

The flight took four and a half hours. When the plane landed in Philadelphia, there was a woman named Mrs. Marquardt waiting for me. She informed me that she was Mr. Jonathon Kim's assistant and that she would be driving me to Blackthorn Academy. She signed some papers from an airline guy to prove that I'd arrived safely, helped me claim my luggage, and then hustled us out the terminal door to the parking garage.

During the drive from the airport, Mrs. Marquardt said not

a word. About fifteen minutes into the trip, I asked her if she was always so talkative. She just kind of grimaced and made a weird chuckling sound but didn't say anything. So the rest of the trip passed in silence.

The landscape south of the Philadelphia airport started to get hilly. Since it was autumn all the trees were turning color, and if you liked that sort of thing it was almost pretty. A little too Amish maybe. But pretty.

A half hour after we left the airport we exited the interstate onto a series of back roads, and fifteen minutes later we pulled through the gates of Blackthorn Academy. Home sweet home.

There was a long drive that went past a little guardhouse, where the guard just waved us through. The car pulled up in front of the building featured on the judge's brochure. It was quite possibly the largest structure I've ever seen. The exterior was made entirely of stainless steel. It was triangular in shape and it looked like one side of the triangle cut back into the side of the mountain. On the side opposite the mountain were a bunch of athletic fields and then a fence with a wooded area beyond that. All of the windows that I could see seemed to be tinted, so you couldn't see inside. I'd have to say that my first impression was that it looked a little creepy. Like the setting for one of those teenage horror slasher movies that come out every summer. The fact that the windows were darkened seemed especially unnerving, and I felt like maybe there were people watching me who didn't want to be seen.

Then again, I have a very active imagination and I always think that I'm the center of the universe, so of course I would think that.

Chatty Mrs. Marquardt instructed me to leave my luggage in the car, and to follow her because Mr. Kim the headmaster was expecting me. Like the building, Mrs. Marquardt also gave me the creeps, with her not talking, the choppy little sentences, and the bossing me around like I was a French poodle. There was something out of whack about her.

But I didn't have much choice, so I followed her through the main door and into a really elaborate and ornate atrium. The space was five stories high, and you could see rooms and hallways leading away from the atrium on the levels above. It was sort of majestic in a way, but also quite empty and a little spooky at the same time. Where were all the juvenile delinquents like me? This had to be the quietest school ever.

"If this is a school, where is everyone?" I asked.

"Class," said the verbose Mrs. Marquardt. "Come."

She marched us across the atrium, through a door at the rear, and down a hallway. We passed dozens of closed doors that looked like classrooms, but saw no one. Again, creeping me out.

Soon we came to an oak door with a gold nameplate on it that said "JONATHON KIM, Headmaster." Mrs. Marquardt knocked, and a cheery voice answered, "Come in."

It all came down to this. I was going to meet my babysitter. My parole officer and warden. The Keeper of Rachel Buchanan. Somehow I'd have to figure out a way to schmooze this guy for the next several months so that I could get out of here. Mrs. Marquardt ushered me through and then left, closing the door behind her. I was three seconds away from meeting the person who would change my life forever.

CHAPTER FOUR

Step off, Mister

Mr. Kim was a pleasant-looking guy. I'd guess he was maybe fifty years old. His hair had been dark and was now speckled with flecks of silver. He was maybe five feet nine and looked like he was pretty fit. He strode across the room toward me and reached out to shake my hand.

"Rachel," he said. "Welcome. We're so glad to have you here." He pumped my hand vigorously and gestured to a chair in front of his desk. As he walked around his desk and sat down facing me, I noticed his desk was completely bare. No papers, no paper clips or pens or anything.

"How was your flight?" he asked.

"Okay, I guess. But that Mrs. Marquardt, what a windbag," I said. There. I'd launched my opening salvo. I wasn't going to make it easy for this guy. Judge "No sense of humor" Kerrigan could lock me up in this dump, but they weren't going to change me. I was going to stay the same Rachel Buchanan.

To my surprise, Mr. Kim laughed. Loudly. And quite enthusiastically.

"That's very funny. Windbag. I will have to remember that. Yes, our Mrs. Marquardt does keep her own counsel. So, Rachel. Tell me why you're here."

"Because I got busted," I said. "But you already know that. Judge Tightass sent me here, like I really had a choice." I don't think Mr. Kim heard the part about me not having a choice, because he was laughing again. This time he slapped the desk with his hand. This was going to be easy. I was killing him! I'd be out of here by the end of the week.

"It's true, the judge is a little bit stern. She was that way when she was a student here. Always very serious. I used to tell her that she needed to lighten up a little, but it just isn't her way. She's very intense."

Wait a minute. Did he say the judge was a student here? She never said anything about that! Shields up!

"Anyway, it was here or Juvie," I said. Still on alert about the "Judge Kerrigan was a student here" bomb. Was that why she was so adamant about sending me to this place?

Mr. Kim looked like he was waiting for me to say something else. But I just started looking at my nails. Wondering if they had a manicurist here at Blackthorn Academy. Finally, he spoke.

"The terms of your arrangement are quite clear. You're part of the Blackthorn family for the next year. You'll be taking a regular class load, doing a work assignment, and studying Tae Kwon Do," he said.

I must have been hallucinating, because I could swear I heard him say something about working and martial arts. No way. Not this chick. I don't do exercise or work.

"I'm sorry, I thought you said Tae Kwon Do. That's like gym. I don't do gym."

He chuckled again, but not as much as he did at my killer "windbag" comment.

"Everyone at Blackthorn does 'gym,' as you call it. It's required in addition to your academic load. We keep busy here. But don't worry. You'll learn to love it. The martial arts are a great way to learn discipline, keep fit, and—"

"Yeah, yeah, yeah," I interrupted him. "I've seen all the Jackie Chan movies. But that's just not my thing. I prefer to spend my free time on other important pursuits. Like TV and junk food," I said. There, that ought to show him.

"Tell me a little about yourself, Rachel," he said. Now, that was a switch. He was changing the subject. I was all ready for a fight, but he was resisting my efforts to pick one. It must be some kind of martial arts "turn your opponent aside gently" thing. Well, two can play at that game. This guy was so easy.

"Not much to tell. Dad from a rich family in Beverly Hills. Made himself a whole bunch richer in real estate or condos or something. Mother bored, depressed, emotionally withdrawn society type, a little too fond of her 'cough medicine,' if you know what I mean," I said.

"But that's about your family," he said. "Tell me about you."

"I don't really like to talk about myself," I said.

"Why not?"

"Well, normally I find me fascinating, but right now I guess I don't care to tell you anything about me." I tried to put just the right amount of hostility in my tone.

"Would you like me to tell you what I know about you?" he asked.

"You don't know anything about me. Look, I'm sure Blackthorn Academy is a four-star boarding school and winner of the National Association of Boarding Schools Gold Award for reprogramming messed-up teenagers or whatever. But I don't want to be here, and nothing you say is going to change my mind. So why don't we get this interview over with so I can get started on my year of exile." I was sure I could just keep talking until I wore this guy down.

"I compliment you on your excellent verbal skills, Rachel. Your attempt to change the subject and try to get me off track is quite impressive. However, I can assure you that I am not so easily dissuaded. I would like to hear more about you, but if you are not comfortable confiding in me at this point, that is completely understandable. Still, would you like to know what I know about you?" Okay, maybe outtalking this guy was going to be harder than I thought.

"You're the guy in charge. Knock yourself out. I really couldn't care less." I wasn't going to let these people get inside my head. They probably brainwashed kids here.

So I pretended not to be completely surprised when Mr. Kim gave me my whole life story. He knew all about my parents, my friends, my grades, what subjects I was good at in school, what my teachers thought of me, that I loved to surf the Internet and write my own computer programs, that my favorite subject, at least until I embarked on my life of crime, was math, that I'd had a dog named Fluffy when I was six, that he'd died when I was eleven. He knew my favorite movie (*Say Anything*), my favorite musical group (Blink 182); he knew all about my probation, the shoplifting, the potential Grand Theft Auto hanging over my head if I didn't stay at this weird place for a year, that I was left-handed, and all about my stupid crush on Boozer. It was a stunning recitation of my entire life, and he repeated it to me with no notes and files. I don't think he even came up for air in the twenty minutes it took him to reduce my life to an oral book report.

I sat there in his office in stunned disbelief. Was he some kind of warlock or something? As far as I knew he hadn't talked to my parents or any of my friends. Charles just signed some papers that Marvin gave him and didn't even say good-bye. I was sure that Charles and Cynthia wouldn't know any of this stuff anyway, even if he did talk to them.

"How did you know all that?" I said.

"Let's just say that I feel it is our duty to know as much about each student as we can. I want you to feel at home here. I realize this is not where you want to be. I expect you to be skeptical, perhaps even hostile. I'm sure I'd feel the same way. It's not easy to be taken out of your home and put in a place where you have no friends and family, not to mention a jail sentence hanging over your head if you don't cooperate."

Empathy? He was going to try the Parenting Handbook, "listen to what your children are really saying and respond with kindness" trick? (I know Charles and Cynthia never tried this, but I saw a parenting show on The Learning Channel once.) *Well, buster,* I thought, *you have met your match.* No one gives me empathy without my permission.

"How nice for you," I said. Okay, not one of my best comebacks, but I was still a little thrown.

"But I want you to understand," Mr. Kim continued. "Judge Kerrigan is not a woman to be crossed. She obviously feels you have a great deal of potential. Many of your friends and teachers that I spoke to felt the same way. And I can tell just by talking to you that you are very smart, with an agile mind. Nonetheless, you will have to embrace our program here at Blackthorn, and it will not be easy. You have many challenges ahead. But from what I've seen so far, I think you will manage them without difficulty."

Okay. First empathy, and then . . . was that last speech a compliment? I had "potential"? An agile mind? No one had ever said that I had an agile anything before. And after two minutes with me he's telling me I'd breeze through the year no problem? Who was this guy?

"Let's walk over to the residential wing and meet your roommate. You'll want to get settled in. Then you'll have a half hour to report to the *do jang* for your first Tae Kwon Do lesson. There is a *do bak*—that's Korean for uniform—in your room already."

He stood up and walked toward the door. By now my head

was spinning. I was tired, homesick, perplexed, and a little pissed off all at the same time. And what was this news flash about a roommate? Nobody had said anything about roommates. I numbly stood up and followed him. No witty comeback. No wisecracks. Whoever this guy was, my first impression had been wrong. He wasn't going to be easy. He was even making me do gym on my first day.

As we walked down another long corridor, my mind was full of so many thoughts that I couldn't grab one to focus on. I noticed now that the school actually looked pretty nice on the inside. Everything was spotlessly clean and the walls were brightly painted. There were lots of pastels and cool colors, like you'd find in a Gap store. If Mr. Kim was in charge of the decorating, I had to give him points for his good color sense.

Mr. Kim's office had been off the atrium, and it seemed now that the interior of the school was laid out like the spokes of a wheel, cut into a quarter section. Hallways led off from the atrium in all directions and the atrium rose up to the full five stories of the school, like something you'd see in a really fancy hotel. That's it. I'd just start thinking of it as a hotel. I wondered if they had room service here.

The hallways looked like they went back quite a ways, and now that I was inside the building I could see that the school was built so that it flowed up the side of the mountain. In the atrium a series of ramps that cut back and forth led to the other floors, and in the hallways every so often there was a doorway marked "Stairs." And as big as the school had looked from the outside, it seemed even bigger once you were inside.

Mr. Kim hummed quietly to himself as we strolled. Now and then we would pass people in the hall, most of them my age, some younger. Apparently I wasn't the only one here after all. Mr. Kim would call each one by name and ask them how they were doing on this glorious day. And the strangest thing was, all of the students seemed to light up when they saw Mr. Kim, like he was a rock star or a celebrity or something. And he made every greeting sound so sincere and genuine.

After we'd walked for a couple of minutes, we rounded a corner and Mr. Kim stopped to say hello to a boy about my age. He was maybe six feet tall with short brown hair and dark eyes. He looked a little like Colin Farrell, actually. Okay, cool colors and cute boys—another point in Blackthorn's favor.

"Brent Christian," said Mr. Kim, "I'd like you to meet our newest student, Rachel Buchanan."

Brent didn't say hi or anything, he just kind of waved at me. I decided not to be rude and waved back.

"Brent is one of our finest students," Mr. Kim said. "I'm sure you will have a lot in common." Brent turned red and looked away. Mr. Kim told him we were on our way to my room. Brent nodded, then just turned and walked away in the direction he'd been going. He hadn't said a word the whole time. I guessed he was probably going off to have a lengthy conversation with Mrs. Marquardt.

Mr. Kim was trying hard to make me feel welcome. And I was doing everything I could to make that as difficult as possible for him. All I could think of was that I wanted to get far away from him and this school as fast as I could. I couldn't picture myself ever being happy to see him in the hallway like the other students. No sir. Not me. I wasn't going to let this guy get to me. I would hold out until I was out of here, and then he could take all of his empathy and praise and little pseudo-parenting tips and use them on the next loser that came through this place.

And the funny thing is, those feelings didn't change all that much for the first couple of weeks that I spent at Blackthorn Academy. Right up until the time Mr. Kim disappeared.

CHAPTER FIVE

Ain't No Party Like a Detroit Party

After what seem liked an hour walk, we finally got to a corridor that led to the girls' wing of the academy. Most of the doors in the corridor were closed, but as we walked past I could hear voices and music. So this place wasn't totally dead. About halfway down the hall, Mr. Kim knocked on a door and swung it open when a voice said to come in.

"Hello, Pilar," said Mr. Kim. "I'd like you to meet your new roommate, Rachel Buchanan." Pilar was tall and slender. She had dark brown curly hair, shoulder length, and beautiful dark brown eyes. She had been sitting at her desk, staring at the door, like she was waiting for us to show up. Okay, not too creepy. She waved to me from where she sat.

"Hi," she said. "Welcome to Blackthorn."

I really didn't know what else to do, so I mumbled a hello and stood there shifting my weight from my left side to my right and back. I looked around the room. It was a two-room suite: a bedroom with two beds and closets in one room, and a study/sitting room with desks and a couple of chairs in the other. Over Pilar's desk was a Blink 182 poster. Okay, that was a good sign. Each of the two rooms had a window, and you could look out of the window and see the athletic fields and the woods beyond. But overall it was small. Very small, compared to home.

Mr. Kim was talking to Pilar about something, so I just kept looking around the room. I saw my suitcase and duffel bag in the bedroom, stacked by one of the closets. At least they hadn't lost my luggage.

"Well, I'll leave you two to get to know each other," Mr. Kim finally said. "We will meet in the *do jang* in thirty minutes. Rachel, your *do bak* is in your closet. Pilar can help you with the belt. See you there."

With that he turned and left. I didn't know what to do. I felt like crying. Pilar looked at me and smiled.

"Don't worry," she said, "I remember how I felt my first day here. It's a little overwhelming. You'll get used to it. The time goes by fast."

"What are you in for?" I asked.

"In for?" she asked.

"Yeah, you know—drugs, stealing, stuff like that?" I said.

She looked puzzled. "I don't understand," she said.

"Didn't the judge in your case send you here?"

A look of understanding came over her face.

"Oh, no—no drugs, no judge. I'm an orphan. My aunt was raising me, but she got sick and couldn't take care of me anymore. A neighbor of ours was a friend of Mr. Kim and knew about Blackthorn, so she arranged for me to get a scholarship. I've been here three years. My aunt passed away last year, so Blackthorn is now my home." She turned around and sat back down at her desk. She had a really sad look on her face, and it made me feel about two inches tall.

So to top off the great day I was having, I had just managed to act like a total jerk to my new roommate. *Someone kill me now.*

"Sorry. I thought . . . never mind. Just . . . I'm sorry," I stammered.

Pilar nodded slightly and returned to reading her book. I took that opportunity to exit stage left and went into the bedroom to unpack my stuff. Despite growing up in BH, I am mostly a jeans and T-shirt kind of girl. I did all my shopping at the Gap and avoided spending too much time on Rodeo Drive. It used to drive Cynthia crazy. "Do you have to dress like a slob?" she'd screech. Funny that she never figured out that the screeching just made me want to dress slobbier.

It took all of ten minutes to stuff all my clothes into the closet and the built-in drawers in the wall. The last thing I pulled out was my laptop, an IBM ThinkPad that Charles had given me for my birthday three months before. Actually, he hadn't really given it to me. He'd given me the money and told me to buy it for myself. He was too busy to shop for my birthday. I loved that laptop—it was probably my most prized possession. But so far I hadn't seen a phone in the room, which probably meant no Internet access. That would cause me to wither and die quicker than anything. I would have to find a way around that somehow.

Pilar came in and opened her closet door. "We don't have phones in our rooms," she said. "You can make calls to your parents from the conference room next to Mr. Kim's office, but you have to reserve a time with Mrs. Marquardt."

"What?" I said.

She pointed to the laptop I held in my hand.

"You were probably wondering where the phone was, and I was just saying we don't have them in our rooms." She stood there watching me with this bizarrely intense expression.

"Is there a problem?" I snapped.

She kind of jumped, like I'd caught her going through my underwear drawer. "No. Uh, sorry. It's just . . . it's nothing really."

"What?" I said. I was still a little cranky from dealing with Mr. Kim, and I needed to get things straight with this chick right away. We had to be roommates, but I didn't have to like it, so she could just step off and give me my space.

"I just feel like I've seen you before. Have you ever been to Detroit, by any chance?"

"No. Ever been to Beverly Hills?" I said it with a rather snotty tone.

"Gosh, no. Is that where you're from?" Gosh? Who the heck says gosh?

"Yeah."

"Cool. Beverly Hills must be awesome. Still, it's weird," she said. "I just have this feeling like I've seen you somewhere."

She began putting on a white martial arts uniform, which fit her like a glove. She pulled a blue belt from a hook inside the closet and fastened it around her waist.

"We better get going. It's a ten-minute walk to the *do jang*, and tardiness means fifty push-ups on your knuckles," she said.

I managed to get the uniform on okay, but the white belt that went with it was hopeless. Pilar stepped over and showed me how to tie it. It looked complicated. It was really bugging me that I had to do this Tae Kwon Do thing. But it couldn't be that hard could it?

"Come on," she said, and we headed out the door.

We walked down a bunch more of those brightly painted corridors (this place seemed like it must be bigger than the Pentagon or something). The Academy residence halls were divided into boys' and girls' wings, with faculty and staff residences in the middle of the two wings, according to Pilar. I hadn't seen any of the classrooms yet.

Finally we entered a room that looked large enough to house a 747. The floor was completely covered with pads and all kinds of punching bags, and other padding hung in different places around the room. At one end of the room a huge American flag was draped on the wall, flanked by a Korean flag of identical size. On the opposite wall was a rack with a lot of long sticks and wooden swords. They looked like they would hurt.

Mr. Kim sat cross-legged on the floor with his back to a line of students lined up down the center of the *do-jang*. At the head of the line were two guys who looked about my age. One wore a black belt. The boy next to him was that Brent kid that Mr. Kim had introduced me to on the way to my room. He had a black stripe on his red belt. The rest of the line was made up of boys and girls of different sizes and ages, and they all had different-colored belts, starting with red after black, then blue, green, yellow, and white.

Pilar whispered quietly to me, "You'll need to line up at the end of the line, with the first gups, the white belts," she said. And she went to the middle of the line with the other blue belts.

I walked to the end of the line and stood next to a boy who looked like he was junior high school age. I towered over him. Everyone was quiet.

Suddenly Mr. Kim sprang to his feet. It happened so fast I almost didn't see it. One minute he was on the floor, back to us, and the next minute he was on his feet facing the line of students.

"Ken yet!" he shouted.

Everyone in the line bowed to him and came to attention. Except me. I just stood there like a lump.

Mr. Kim walked over to me and smiled. "Class," he said, "please welcome our newest student, Ms. Buchanan."

All the students said *"kyun in sepsido"* all at the same time.

Mr. Kim smiled. "That means welcome in Korean," he said.

He stood in front of me and showed me how to come to attention. Feet together, back straight, arms by my side, extended at a slight angle.

"All right. Mr. Scott, please warm up the class," he said.

The black-belt guy bowed and then walked to where Mr. Kim had been sitting. He turned to the class and shouted, "Jumping jacks!" He started counting in Korean and doing the jumping jacks. Mr. Kim looked at me, and I began a halfhearted attempt at following along. Mostly doing the jumping without the jack.

We quickly went on to push-ups and a series of stretches. After the push-ups I was sweating and my legs and arms were quivering. Finally the exercises stopped and Mr. Scott gave instructions for the class to break up into groups by rank and work on "self-defense." Great. More gym.

"Come with me, Ms. Buchanan," Mr. Kim said.

He walked with me across the *do jang* to where Mr. Scott stood watching some younger students pretend-punch each other. Mr. Scott was tall, over six feet, and his blond hair was cut short and close to his scalp. He was definitely ripped. Now that I could see him up close, I could see that he was maybe sixteen or seventeen. And he wasn't bad to look at.

He said something in what must have been Korean, and they stopped what they were doing. "Try it like this," he said.

He stepped onto the mat and the three lower belts formed a triangle around him. One of them held a small wooden club about two feet long. He came at Mr. Scott with an overhead swing. At about half speed Mr. Scott blocked the downward arc of the club and twisted the blue belt's arm behind his back. While he moved he carefully explained each technique to the students. He softly kicked the back of his attacker's knee and the blue belt dropped to the ground, losing the club in the process. Mr. Scott whisked the club away with a flick of his foot as the other two blue belts descended on him. He took out one blue belt with a pretend kick to the stomach and the third one with some kind of fancy spin-around kick that, had he been going full steam, would have taken out the guy's legs. Amazingly, even though it was a demonstration, he seemed to move really fast. He straightened his *do bak* and addressed the students.

"Remember, the attacker with the weapon is the first priority. Also, if you can, once you have disarmed the attacker, either use the weapon yourself or kick it away. Don't let one of the others grab it and get a chance to use it on you again."

Mr. Scott gave them another command in Korean and they returned to their exercise.

He turned as we approached and bowed, which Mr. Kim returned.

"Mr. Alex Scott, this is Ms. Buchanan," he said. The guy turned and bowed in my direction. I kind of nodded and said, "Hey, how's it goin'?"

"You must return the bow," Mr. Kim said. He showed me how to cross my arms in front of me and bow. It took me about four times to get it right. I noticed Mr. Scott had a smirk on his face as he watched me.

"What's so funny, muscle head?" I glared at him.

"Ms. Buchanan," Mr. Kim said quietly, "in the *do jang,* during class, or in competition we address each other as 'Mr.' or 'Ms.', not 'muscle head.' When you address me or Mr. Torres, whom you will meet tomorrow, you address us as 'Master.'"

"Why?" Like that was going to happen. Me call somebody *master*? Keep dreaming, Mr. Kim.

Mr. Scott spoke up. "Master Kim, may I?" Mr. Kim nodded.

Alex looked at me and bowed again. "Master Kim is a ninth Dan in the art of Tae Kwon Do. It is the highest rank that can be achieved in the art and takes years to earn. Mr. Torres is a fifth Dan. When a student earns the rank of fourth Dan, they earn the right to be called Master. Each Dan, or rank, is noted on the uniform, by the stripes on the *do bak*. I am a second Dan black belt."

I looked at Mr. Kim's uniform and noticed the difference. Mr. Scott's black belt looked relatively new and stiff compared to Mr. Kim's, which was faded and looked like it had been through the wash a few times. Mr. Kim's uniform top was hemmed with black stripes, and there were several thin black stripes running down his pant legs. Alex's *do bak* had only a single black stripe running down the pant leg.

"Oh," I said. I was the queen of the witty comeback, after all.

"Mr. Scott, please begin Ms. Buchanan's study of the first pattern."

They bowed to each other, and Mr. Kim turned to another group of students.

"Follow me," Alex said.

We went over to a fairly deserted corner of the room and Mr. Scott began introducing me to the art of Tae Kwon Do. First I had to learn a "sound-off," which gave the history and meaning of the first pattern. Learning stuff by memory is pretty easy for me. There was a lot of stuff in the sound-off about kings and dynasties and Buddhist monks. It took only a few times through the sound-off, before I had memorized all the words. But the physical part was impossible. There were too many movements, and Mr. Scott kept stopping me and showing me how to do it correctly. Once when I fell sprawling to the mat he couldn't stifle a chuckle.

"You think this is funny?" I snapped.

"Honestly, yeah. You were kind of all over the place on that one. But don't worry, you'll catch on." He was totally giving me attitude. I was about to let him have it, but I noticed that his eyes, which were a steel-gray color, were kind of laughing too, and I momentarily forgot my witty retort. Did I mention he was devastatingly cute?

But I couldn't get the moves at all. Just when I felt like I was about to cry, Mr. Kim shouted another command and the class stopped. Everyone bowed to one another and went back to the line the class started in. I stood at the end again. Mr. Kim said a bunch of other stuff, the class turned to face the flags on the wall, and everybody recited the Student Oath of Tae Kwon Do: "Courtesy. Integrity. Perseverance. Self-control. Indomitable Spirit." All of which are qualities that I don't possess, by the way.

"Class dismissed. Ms. Buchanan, a moment, please," Mr. Kim said.

As the students filed out, Mr. Kim came over to where I stood.

"I will have some study material brought to your room. Do not be discouraged. Tae Kwon Do is a difficult and challenging art. But the rewards it offers are immense. You had a good first class. It will get easier each time."

"I can't do this," I said. "I'm no good at gym stuff. Isn't there something else I can do instead?"

Mr. Kim smiled and bowed his head for a moment.

"Ms. Buchanan. Look at all that you've accomplished in the last twenty-four hours. You've left your home and flown across the country, matched wits with Mrs. Marquardt, enrolled in a new school, met a new roommate, and finished a first class in what is a difficult and very challenging physical discipline. You have a great deal to be proud of. You must give yourself credit."

"But I can't do it. It's too complicated. I am a thinker, not a doer." Yeah, it was definitely my great thinking that got me here in the first place.

"You are right. As I have said, you have an agile mind. That is why you will easily master Tae Kwon Do. Tae Kwon Do is all about thinking. Doing comes second. Think first and you will become a fine martial artist."

I was exhausted and (for once) tired of talking. The more I was around Mr. Kim, the more it became apparent that he had an answer for everything. I wanted out of here. I missed Boozer and Jamie and Grego—heck, I was even starting to miss Charles and Cynthia. At least they didn't make me do gym. I hated this place. I wanted to go home. But I had nothing left to say. So I just turned and walked away, leaving Mr. Kim standing alone in the *do jang*.

CHAPTER SIX

The First Train Out of Here

I got lost twice trying to find my way back to my room. I was now convinced this place had to be bigger on the inside than it looked on the outside. There were corridors and hallways all over the place. Finally I figured out that the corridors were all color-coded. There was a yellow corridor leading away from the *do jang* in one direction, which must be where the classrooms were. Then there was a blue corridor that led back to the atrium and the offices, which led to the rust and mauve corridors that went to the boys' and girls' wings.

Pilar was at her desk again when I finally got back.

"Do you want to go to the cafeteria for dinner?" she asked.

"No. Thanks." What I felt like doing was running away.

Pilar just looked at me. On the one hand, I felt kind of bad about what I'd said to her before. She seemed okay. But on the other hand, she kept staring at me all the time when she thought I wasn't looking. Like I was a bug she wanted to dissect or something. It was mega-creepy. She started to the door of the room and then stopped.

"Are you sure? I think you should take a shower and then come to the cafeteria with me. Have dinner. Meet some of the other students. What can it hurt?"

"Thanks. Really. But I'm not hungry." She stood there staring at me again. It was starting to creep me out. "Look, I'm really tired and I've had a long day. Do you think you could can the staring act?"

"I'm sorry," she said. "You're right, it's rude of me. But I can't tell you how strong this feeling is that I know you somehow."

"Yeah, well, I don't care. I don't know you. You don't know me. We've established that I've never been to Detroit and you've never been to BH. So why don't you give it a rest?"

"I'm sorry," she said again. She gave an embarrassed shrug and left the room.

I went into the bedroom and took my duffel bag out of the closet. I threw in some of my clothes and the $200 in cash that I had stuck in one of my socks. I grabbed my laptop and stuffed it in the duffel bag. I changed clothes and threw the *do bak* in the closet. I was getting out of here. A whole year of this? It just wasn't worth it.

Maybe I could get a bus ticket back to California and crash at Boozer's for a while. Boozer lived with his dad, who was gone on business all the time. No one would find me there. And even if they did, I didn't care. Judge Tightass could send me to Juvie, for all I cared. At least I wouldn't have to make a fool of myself doing stupid martial arts. I shoved the duffel bag under my bunk.

Pilar came back from dinner about forty-five minutes later. I had to come up with a plan to get out of here, but first I needed information. But I had to be careful. I didn't want her squealing on me.

"So, Pilar, what do you do around here at night?"

"Study," she said. "Classes are tough, and I've got to really buckle down."

"Ha. Really? You don't hang out at the mall or anything?"

"We're in the middle of nowhere, and there isn't a mall for miles. How would we go to a mall?" It wasn't like she was being snippy or anything. It was just like the idea of going to the mall had never occurred to her.

"Okay. I was just asking. Isn't there a rec room or someplace with a TV?"

"There is a rec room in Yellow corridor with Ping-Pong and stuff, but no TV. Mr. Kim is not a fan of TV."

I *knew* I didn't like him.

"What if I want to go for a walk or something?"

"You can walk around the grounds. Sometimes we go outside and run on the track or play softball or touch football on the athletic fields."

Great. More gym. Who were these people?

Pilar looked at me again for a few seconds, and then she said something that gave me the chills.

"Listen," Pilar said. "I'm not stupid. I know what kind of walk you're thinking about. Almost everybody goes for a walk within the first couple of days here." When she said "walk," of course she made the little "air quote" sign. I wanted to scream and run. "But it's better for you if you don't try it."

"Try what?" I said, not believing that she could figure me out that easily.

"Running away. It's not a good idea."

"I'm not running away."

"Sure you are. Everyone tries it when they first get here. But you can't get past the guardhouse at the front gate. You're not in good enough shape to make it over the fence around the front of the school, and as for the woods, well, they're thick and confusing and you don't want to try them at night."

Not in good enough shape? Ouch.

"Look," I said. "I don't know what you think you know about me. But I was just trying to make conversation. You know, learn about this place. I don't know where you got this 'me running away' drama." Of course, none of that was even remotely true. My desire to get out of there must have been plastered on my face, because she had me pegged.

"Okay. Whatever." She turned her back to me, sat down at her desk, and opened a book.

I went into the bedroom and crawled into my bunk. She couldn't have known what I was thinking. And that creepy, staring-at-me thing, like she knew me. Maybe Mr. Kim roomed me with her on purpose, to teach me a lesson. Maybe this school was really like Juvie and she was going to beat me up in my sleep or something. That sealed it. I was definitely getting out of here. But I had to wait for her to go to sleep.

I was tired and it was hard to stay awake, but I was determined. Finally, after what seemed like several hours of studying, Pilar came into the room, changed into pajamas, and got into bed.

I pretended to be sleeping. I heard her tossing and turning a little bit, and then after a while she seemed to settle down and I could hear her breathing even out and get deeper. She started to mutter a little in her sleep. I waited several more minutes, as she continued to breathe and mutter and mumble. I was pretty sure she was asleep. I sat up and put my feet on the floor.

"Good luck, Rachel," she said all at once, clear as day. I froze in place.

Good luck? Had she heard me? Was she just being a smart-ass? Or was she some kind of psychic? My skin was crawling with goose bumps. I sat completely still and waited. She kept muttering strange-sounding words and phrases that didn't make any sense. I waited long enough to know that she had to be sleeping. Creepy.

I quickly got up off the bed, grabbed my duffel, and crept to the door. I very carefully pulled it open and stepped through into the hallway. Everything was quiet. So far, so good.

I headed down the hallway toward the shower room. I figured that there wouldn't be any alarms or motion detectors in the main hallway here, in case people needed to use the bathroom during the night. But once I moved out into the connecting hallway I was going to have to be careful. There were probably all kinds of alarms and motion detectors and stuff. The place was full of juvenile delinquents, after all.

The lights in the hall were low for nighttime. When I reached the end of the hall, I stopped. I reached into the duffel bag and pulled out my bottle of Nivea Bath Powder. I had seen this trick in the movie *Entrapment,* with Catherine Zeta-Jones. I squirted a big puff of powder up and down out into the hallway. If there were motion detectors or sensors, the electronic beams would be illuminated in the powder.

That's funny. Nothing. I was surprised. Maybe they used invisible beams. But if a beam was invisible then it really wasn't a beam, was it? Did they have something more sophisticated? Only one way to find out.

I turned into the hallway. Nothing happened. No shrieking alarms. No Doberman pinschers came barreling out of nowhere. Weird. This wasn't much of a jail so far. I headed quickly down the hallway.

The academy was so danged big, I got lost about three times. But I had a general sense of where the atrium was, and eventually, after a couple of wrong turns, I found it. It was deserted. I went to the main door and looked out at the front gate of the school. Dang! There was a security guard in the guardhouse. It must be manned around the clock. I was going to have to find another way out.

I headed all the way back through the school to the *do jang.* There were no windows, and only one door with a sticker on it saying "Fire alarm, do not open except in an emergency." D'oh! I headed back out and down the yellow corridor leading toward the classrooms.

It was very quiet and kind of creepy prowling around the school at night with everyone asleep. I tried the door on one of the classrooms and was surprised to find it unlocked. Inside, it wasn't like any classroom I'd ever been in. Instead of desks it was full of what looked like incredibly comfortable reclining easy chairs. At the front of the room, instead of a blackboard, there was a really big TV or computer monitor of some kind that was built into the wall. What the heck? I thought Pilar said Mr. Kim wasn't a fan of TV. But I didn't have time to think about it.

I hurried across the room to the windows. They had a handle that you pushed aside to open them outward. I looked the window over carefully and didn't see any wires or anything that indicated it might be alarmed. Cautiously I pushed it open and peered out into the night.

I was on the other side of the school now, away from the guardhouse, and facing what looked like a bunch of athletic fields with the woods off in the distance. This was my way out!

Only one problem. Somehow this room was on the second floor. The corridor that led here must have sloped upward into the side of the hill, but I hadn't noticed it.

I really hate this place, I thought to myself.

I was running out of time. I could try to find another way out, but the longer I stayed inside the more I risked getting caught. I looked down and noticed that there was a ledge below the window, leading to a steel downspout that led to the ground. Maybe I would be able to shimmy down that somehow. Yeah, me shimmy. I'd already had enough gym for a week.

But I didn't see another option. I dropped my bag out the

window and it landed on the grass with a quiet thud. I stepped up onto the radiator in front of the window and climbed out on the ledge, which was not as wide as it looked—maybe about six inches. My feet barely fit on it. I nearly fell when I took my first step toward the downspout. Once I steadied myself, I kept inching along the ledge carefully until I got to it. But then I had a problem. My back was to the wall, and if I was going to shimmy down, I was going to have to turn around somehow and grab the downspout with both hands.

Come on, Rachel, I thought. *They do this kind of stuff in movies all the time. How hard can it be?*

Pretty darn hard, let me tell you. I reached up and grabbed the downspout with my right hand. I held it as tight as I could and then took my left foot and tried to swing it around so that I could straddle the downspout. That's when it all went bad. All of my weight shifted forward and I started to fall. I grabbed tighter with my right hand and tried to swing myself around quickly, but I missed the ledge with my left foot and couldn't dig into the wall with my toes. I grabbed the downspout with my left hand, but when I did my weight shifted again and my right foot slipped off the ledge.

I hung there trying to get my feet back up on the ledge, but I didn't have the strength or the coordination to do it. My arms and hands started to cramp and quiver from the strain. I tried to hand-over-hand my way down the downspout, but I got only about two feet before I couldn't hang on anymore and my hands let go.

I was falling.

CHAPTER SEVEN

Falling With Style

I must have had the wind knocked out of me. I don't think I actually lost consciousness. From my position flat on my back, I looked up at the ledge and calculated that I had fallen maybe ten feet. I'd whacked my head pretty hard on the ground, but the grass was soft and even though I didn't feel like I could move very well yet, I didn't seem to be seriously injured. What a miracle.

I started to laugh. Remember that weird nervous laugh I have when I'm scared or excited? I couldn't help it. It just struck me as funny. What the heck was I doing? Oh yeah, escaping. For a moment I stopped to look at the night sky. It was cloudless and there was a full moon. It was beautiful. If I hadn't felt like I had just been run over by a truck, I would have enjoyed it.

Slowly I started to stand up. Whoa. Big mistake. Woozy. I lay back down and waited for the spinning to stop. When it did, I sat up. Better. I was kind of numb all over. My arms and legs seemed to work, but my right wrist was sore, like I'd sprained it. I must have stuck it out to try to stop my fall. I'd have to take it easy.

I stood up and tried to get my bearings. That's when I noticed that there was a door in front of me that led back into the school. I hadn't been able to see it from the window above. It was probably locked anyway. I peered in the window at the frame of the door, and I didn't see any alarm boxes or wires, so it didn't look like a fire door. But I decided not to chance opening it anyway. All I needed was to set off the alarms at this point.

I was now on the side of Blackthorn Academy facing out from the mountain. No one should be able to see me from the front. All of the athletic fields lay beyond me for several hundred yards. There was a track, a football field, and a couple of baseball or softball diamonds. They were all deserted with not a soul in sight. Beyond them lay probably the thickest woods I'd ever seen in my life.

I figured I'd go over the chain-link fence and into the woods. Then I'd head back toward the road, keeping the school in sight so I didn't get lost, until I hit the freeway. Then I could hitch a ride. Of course, I'd never hitched a ride before, but I'd read about it. You stick out your thumb, somebody stops (hopefully not a crazed psycho traveling serial killer), and you've got your ride. What could go wrong?

I walked all the way across the fields until I came to the fence, which was about eight feet high. I had no idea how I was going to get over it. I kept thinking about Pilar's crack about me not being in good enough shape to get out. But I'd show *her*. In police shows on TV you see people climb these fences all the time when they are being chased. They just run at it and scamper over like monkeys. So it couldn't be too hard. I shifted my duffel bag around so it was on my back, then backed up a few feet, ran at the fence, and jumped. I bounced off the fence and landed on my butt, digging my sore wrist into the ground. Yow!

Not to be deterred, I tried it again. I didn't fall down immediately this time, but I couldn't get a grip on the fence with my sore wrist and I couldn't get my feet to dig in and push me up. Eventually I slipped and fell again, this time landing against the fence. This wasn't going to work.

The fence wound all the way around the complex until it hooked back up with the school on both ends. I didn't see any gates nearby, but they would all be locked anyway.

What to do? Giving up was not an option. I tried to run through some other escape scenarios in my head: (1) Hide in a laundry cart and get loaded on a truck and sneak out the back door when the truck stops. Okay, could work. Except I had the feeling that Mr. Kim probably made everybody at Blackthorn wash their own clothes on the rocks in a nearby stream, so there probably wouldn't be a laundry truck. (2) I could steal a spoon from the cafeteria and tunnel my way to freedom. (3) I could pretend to be sick and get taken to a hospital and escape from there, but what if they had some kind of medical ward in the school where they stuck me? Besides, those plans would keep me here for at least another day, and I wanted out now. There had to be a way.

Just then I noticed that the baseball field had some wooden benches along the baselines where the players sat. Hmmm. If I could drag one of them over here, maybe I could prop it up on top of the fence and shimmy my way over.

I left my duffel bag by the fence and trotted over to the bench. It was probably fifteen feet long and made of aluminum with wooden legs. Still, it was heavy, and I had to turn it upside down and drag it the hundred yards or so back to the fence. Not so easy when you've got a probably sprained wrist and are extremely sore from having to do gym for the first time in years. Finally I managed to wrestle it up on its end and tip it toward the fence. The legs on that end of the bench hooked over the top of the fence, and bingo, I had a ramp.

Now I just needed to climb it. It was steep and the aluminum was slippery. I shifted my duffel around so it was on my back again, then started up the bench and immediately slipped back down. I tried again, with the same result. This was hard! Sometimes you just can't escape from a boarding school.

This called for desperate action. I could see only one way to make it over. I backed up and took a running start straight up the bench. I almost stumbled near the top, but I pushed harder with my legs and gave myself a boost. I flew off the end of the bench, and the next thing I knew I was soaring through the air.

I didn't land perfectly, but it was better than I did coming down off the ledge. My wrist hit the ground again and I yelped in pain. But I was over!

I stood up and looked around the woods. There were creepy-looking Wizard of Oz trees all over this forest, and it was very dark. Dark like the kind of woods that Jamie Lee Curtis runs through in the *Halloween* movies when she's being chased by the evil Michael Myers. I glanced back at the school and the bench lying on the fence. In the morning, they would know for sure this was how I had escaped, but I planned to be long gone by then. I took a deep breath and looked at the woods again.

What I was really doing was stalling. I don't like woods. I'm not a woods person. Bad things happen in woods. Any episode of Scooby-Doo will tell you that. And this, as I've said, was a particularly scary-looking wood. I don't know what kind of trees they were, but they were thick and overgrown and the branches hung low to the ground. Branches that would undoubtedly reach out and grab you as you walked by.

I decided to follow the fence for as long as I could and keep the school in sight. Since eventually I'd be back around to the front of the school and in sight of the guardhouse, I was going to have to cut into the woods at some point. But I'd worry about that later.

I started along the fencerow and was about fifty yards from where I'd jumped it when I found a gate. An unlocked gate. A totally and completely unlocked, open-me-up-and-walk-right-through-me gate. I hadn't noticed it in the darkness.

So I'd nearly broken my neck and killed myself twice for no good reason. I bet that stupid door I saw back at the building was wide open too. Stupid school! It almost made me want to go back and wake Mr. Kim up and give him a stern lecture about security. This school was supposed to be full of "bad seeds" like me! How could he go around leaving things open all the time?

I kept walking along the fence, but before I got back to the front of the school I ran into a problem: an enormous ravine. From the fence it led away into the woods. The side where I stood had a more gentle slope down, but the opposite side went almost straight up. It looked much too steep to climb.

I could go back through the gate, try the front entrance, and hope the guard was asleep. Or I could try to follow this ravine into the woods and cut back around to the road. I didn't like option B, but I'd already been at this for an hour and I was going to lose a lot of time if I went back.

So I scrambled down the side of the ravine and headed into the woods. This was a strange and twisty ravine. It twisted around and cut back and forth and led down deeper into the woods. It must have been some kind of weird geological thing from the mountain. The trees kept getting thicker, and pretty soon the moon was blocked out so it was really dark. I reached into the pocket of my duffel and pulled out the little mini-Maglite that I had packed before I left. The flashlight cut the darkness a little, but not much, and it was still spooky. I could hear things rustling in the woods and scampering around in the underbrush.

Once I heard a horrible screech that nearly made me jump out of my skin. After my heart rate returned to normal, I did a very fast and convincing job of telling myself that it was just an owl. Of course, being from Beverly Hills, I know nothing about owls and for all I know it could have been the Blair Witch after me. But saying "it's only an owl" sixty-seven times made me feel better.

Soon I came out of the ravine and the woods flattened out before me. Now I had another problem. The ravine, with its winding course, had left me totally lost with no sense of which way I needed to go to reach the road. I couldn't see the moon through the thick trees, and I had gone far enough into the woods that I couldn't see the school either. I thought I needed to head to my right to reach the road, but I couldn't be sure . . . maybe it was my left. Maybe I could have figured it out if I had a compass. Of course, I didn't know how to read a compass, but if I had one, at least I'd look professional as I got more and more lost. Then, when they found my body in the woods, dead fingers clutched around the compass, they'd say, "Ooh, that's what happened. She headed south/southeast instead of due west."

Even when I'm about to die, I crack myself up.

There was only one decision as far as I was concerned. Pick a direction and go. I was in eastern Pennsylvania, not Siberia, so eventually I'd run into a road somewhere. Or so I thought. Except the trees made it hard to go straight, and there were a lot of thick bushes and big rocks that I had to go around. So I went as straight as I could, which was not very straight at all, and I walked for what must have been another hour, and I was still no closer to anywhere civilized as far as I could see.

I felt like I wanted to cry again. I hadn't cried since I was eleven and Fluffy died. But ever since my trial it seemed like all I wanted to do was cry. *I'm not a crier. I am a witty and intelligent young woman with a bright future,* I told myself. But I felt like crying anyway. I was exhausted, lost, and out of ideas.

My flashlight battery was starting to go dim, and I had not brought a spare. *Great planning, Rachel.* I decided I needed to rest for a few minutes, so I sat on the ground by a giant boulder and leaned my head back. I reached into my duffel and pulled out my white UCLA sweatshirt and shucked it on. It was still early autumn, but it was getting colder. The boulder felt cool against my neck and head, and that was soothing. I tried to clear my mind. I'd have a good idea any second, I was sure.

Instead, of course, I fell asleep.

And I had the strangest dream. I almost never dream when I sleep, or if I do, I never remember them. But I remembered this one. I was running down a hallway or a corridor, or it might have been the ravine in the woods. Someone was chasing me. He wore some kind of large golden medallion around his neck, and for a second I could swear that his head turned into the head of a bull, with giant horns sticking out the side. He was getting closer and closer. I kept running and turning corners and trying to get away from him.

I turned a corner and ran into a large storeroom that was filled with big boxes or crates. Except that the crates weren't really crates. They might have been boulders like the ones in the woods. I ran back and forth among the crates, trying to find a place to hide. Finally I huddled on the ground next to this big crate, only it wasn't a crate, it was the boulder I was sitting next to in the woods. And I looked up, and then I saw the weird face of the man/bull above me and I thought, *How did he get above me?* And then he said, "Good morning Rachel!" And I awoke with a shout and jumped to my feet and looked up into the smiling face of Mr. Kim, sitting cross-legged on the boulder.

CHAPTER EIGHT

I'm Sure You're a Nice Person, but This Just Isn't Going to Work

"You just scared the bejabbers out of me!" I yelled.

"I'm sorry, Rachel. I didn't mean to startle you. I didn't want to frighten you, so I let you sleep for a while. You did an amazing job getting out of the school, I must say. No one has ever thought to use a bench as a ramp over the back fence. Most new students try to sneak past the guardhouse, but Mr. Henderson usually catches them. It's been a long time since somebody has tried to leave here through the woods."

I didn't know what to say. I was tired and sore. I'd had a strange dream, and this Kim guy really had a way of keeping me off guard. Every time I expected him to yell at me for something, he would tell me how smart I was and what a good job I'd done. If Judge Kerrigan or Charles or Cynthia had been sitting on that rock, I'd be in Juvie now or worse. But this guy, even when it seemed like you should be punished, gave you a compliment. What was up with that? It was really starting to tick me off. And that dream was still disturbing me a little. I looked around and saw that it was lighter out. The moon was down, so it must have been early morning. I felt completely out of sorts.

"Were you planning on heading back to California?" he asked.

"No," I lied. "Just away, you know, anywhere but here."

Mr. Kim nodded but didn't say anything.

"I'm not going back to that school," I said. "You can't make me."

"No. You are correct. I can't force you. Even if I could, I can sense from your determined spirit that you would keep trying until you succeeded in getting away from the school. However, I would prefer you not hitchhike anywhere. If you wish, I will drive you to the airport and get you safely on a flight back to Los Angeles."

"I told you, I'm not going back to Los Angeles," I lied again. I figured deception would throw him off the track. "That stupid judge would just send me to Juvie."

"Yes, she would. But perhaps you have someone you could stay with for a while. Maybe your friend Boozer? He might be willing to take you in, wouldn't he?"

Now I was freaked. This guy was like Yoda or something. He had my plan figured out practically before I did. Plus offering to drive me to the airport, and then basically telling me to run away and hang with Boozer? This guy obviously didn't understand that his job was to crack down on delinquents like me. He should have been dragging me back to Blackthorn and putting me in solitary confinement or something.

"Uh. No. Boozer wouldn't do that." I lied again.

"Ah. Well, you're a smart girl. You'll think of something. But at any rate, let me offer a compromise. If you wish, I will take you to the airport now. However, if you return with me to Blackthorn, I promise you there will be no recriminations and no mention of this to your parents or Judge Kerrigan. Agree to stay for one month. Thirty days is all I ask. At the end of the month we'll talk, and if you still wish to leave, I'll put you on the plane to L.A. and what you do when you get there will be your business. If you can elude Judge Kerrigan and her storm troopers, well, that will be up to you. Of course, you realize you could end up in Juvenile Detention. I assure you Judge Kerrigan is not a big believer in second chances. But I am. So, what do you say?"

I was now officially overwhelmed. He was kidding, right? Storm troopers?

"How do I know you won't keep me at the school against my will?"

"You don't. You'll just have to trust me."

Trust. Hah. People are always saying "trust me." I didn't trust anybody but good old Rachel Buchanan. I hadn't met many people that you could trust. I certainly couldn't trust Charles and Cynthia to act like parents. None of my teachers ever seemed real interested in helping me out. And Boozer, he was fun, but not really someone you could trust when it came down to it. About the only adult I'd ever met that I thought I might be able to trust, believe it or not, was Judge Kerrigan, and

I only trusted her to toss me in the hoosegow if I didn't go to this stupid school. And now here was jolly Mr. Kim saying "trust me."

"Rachel. Please. Give us a chance. Let me help you," Mr. Kim said. He sounded very sincere.

Right then I felt tired and a lot older than fifteen. No matter what I tried, it didn't seem like there was any way out of this whole stupid idea. Suddenly it seemed easier to go back to the Academy and do the stupid Tae Kwon Do and stuff and just get the year over with. I choked back tears and nodded.

"Thank you, Rachel. I will do my best to see that you are not disappointed with this decision."

He jumped down from the boulder, smiling.

"Follow me," he said. He led me over a little rise and through some thick trees, and in about thirty yards we were back at the gate in the fence. It figured. Mr. Kim pulled the gate open and we walked right through it.

We didn't talk until we were almost back to the school.

"Mr. Kim, how did you know where to find me?"

"Your trail was fairly easy to follow. Using the bath powder to check for motion detectors was very smart. But you left powder footprints—first leading to the atrium, and again headed toward the *do jang* when you came back. The window in classroom 221 was open and there was a depression in the ground below where you must have landed when you fell. Are you injured?"

"My wrist is sore and my pride is damaged, but I think I'm okay."

"Then I tracked you through the woods and found you

asleep by the rock. And here we are."

I stopped for a minute and looked back the way we had come. Off in the distance I could see the bench still leaning up against the fence.

"You know, I'm never going to get this Tae Kwon Do stuff."

"We will work on that. The important thing is that you try. You respond well to challenges, Rachel. Give yourself a chance. As I said, you're not the first student to try running away on the first day. Mr. Scott, Mr. Christian, Pilar, even Judge Kerrigan have all taken similar walks like this with me."

I couldn't stifle a laugh. "Judge Kerrigan! A runaway? You're totally kidding me!"

"No. Theresa had, shall we say, an enormously bad attitude when she got here. I remember she arrived in the morning and was headed to the freeway by a little after midnight. She tried to go through the woods, same as you. I found her in almost the same spot, in fact."

Well. Sometimes life surprises you. Judge "Hair in an Unfashionable Bun" Kerrigan had run away from Blackthorn too. Now, *that* was funny. "This school will do wonders for you," she'd said. Yeah, right.

I looked back at the woods and suddenly remembered the dream again. A chill ran through me, and I shuddered.

Mr. Kim looked at me. "Rachel, is there something else? Are you feeling ill?"

"What? Oh. No. I was just thinking. I had this really weird dream when I was sleeping out there, and it kind of shook me up."

Mr. Kim seemed to relax. "Really?" he said. "Dreams can be

very interesting. What was yours about?" We had reached the back of the school now and were walking up to the door that I had wondered about last night. Sure enough, Mr. Kim reached out and pulled it open. No alarm. No lock. No nothing. Sheesh. He stopped to hold it open for me.

"I dreamed I was running down a long corridor and there was a guy chasing me. Only the corridor kept changing, and sometimes it was the hallway of the school, sometimes it was the hallway of someplace I didn't recognize, and sometimes it was the ravine in the woods. And the man was strange. He wore a really big gold medallion around his neck and his head kept changing. For a moment, I could have sworn he turned into a bull and not a man."

I had kept walking while I was talking, and I didn't notice that Mr. Kim had stopped dead. When I turned around he was holding the door and staring at me with the strangest expression. The color was completely drained from his face.

"What did you say? About him changing?" He was gripping the door so hard his knuckles were turning white.

"He turned into a bull. Or at least his head did. It grew horns and he looked like a bull. And he was chasing me."

"Did he say anything to you in the dream?"

"I don't remember. Why? It's just some crazy dream."

That seemed to snap Mr. Kim out of it. He shook his head as if he were clearing his thoughts.

"It's nothing. It's a strange-sounding dream, that's all. Let's get you back to your room. You've got class this morning."

Something in the way Mr. Kim was acting had me on alert.

Most of the time I'm happy to go along with my preferred idea that everything in the world revolves around me. But ever since I'd come across Judge Kerrigan and arrived at this school, people were treating me oddly. Pilar kept staring at me all the time and saying she felt like she knew me from somewhere. Then, when I thought about it, I remembered Mrs. Marquardt spending a lot of time watching me in the rearview mirror on the drive from the airport.

I mean, I guess it's normal that when somebody new arrives, you check them out. And yet this felt different. Mr. Kim was definitely upset somehow. I had a sense that something was going on, even if I didn't know what yet. But I would find out.

Mr. Kim took me through a hallway. As we were about to turn up the stairs, I noticed a red door with a sign that said "Top Floor. Access Restricted. Top Floor Students & Faculty Only Beyond This Point."

"What's a 'top floor student'?" I asked.

Mr. Kim was still thinking about something.

"Hmmm? Oh, the Top Floor is a special classroom wing of the school for the upper classes. It's where Blackthorn students who show special aptitudes in various areas of study take advanced classes. We call them Top Floor Students."

"That sounds cool. What kind of classes?"

"Various kinds. We need to stop by the infirmary and have your wrist checked out."

Why did I feel like Mr. Kim was changing the subject?

"What do you have to do to become a Top Floor Student?" I asked.

"There are a variety of standards. You shouldn't concern yourself too much with it yet, Rachel. I've known you barely twenty-four hours and I have no doubt you'll be running the school in a few short weeks. You'll be able to learn all about it then."

At the infirmary, the nurse took an X-ray and confirmed that my wrist was only sprained. She wrapped it in an Ace bandage and gave me some Advil. Mr. Kim showed me how to get back to my room from there.

When I came in, Pilar was still sleeping. I put my duffel bag on my bed and kicked off my shoes. I went back out and down the hall to the shower room, which turned out to be awesome. It was decorated with brightly colored ceramic tiles, and there were cabinets built into the wall with big fluffy towels and an open closet that held big bathrobes. I peeled off my clothes and stepped into the shower. It felt great. I was still tired and very sore. Inside the shower stall was a little holder with disposable toothbrushes, and a shampoo, toothpaste, and conditioner dispenser were lined up under the showerhead. Pretty slick. I washed my hair and brushed my teeth and started to feel better. Not happy. But better. Maybe if I stayed in the shower room the whole year, everything would be just fine.

CHAPTER NINE

This Must Be a Month in Dog Years

When I got back to the room, Pilar was awake and sitting at her desk, going over notes. Did she ever not study?

I went into the other room, dried my hair, dressed, and unpacked my laptop.

"How did it go?" Pilar asked as I carried the laptop back into the study room and sat down at my desk.

"How'd what go?"

"Your 'walk.'" Air quotes again. I was definitely going to kill her.

"Not so well. Got lost in the woods."

"How'd you get back?"

"Mr. Kim seemed to have no trouble finding me."

"Yeah, he's like that. Wow. The woods. Pretty brave."

I couldn't tell if she was teasing me or what. I decided not to press it and started opening the drawers of my desk. Inside the top drawer was a manila envelope with a sticker on it that said "Rachel Buchanan: Class Schedule." I opened it and looked at the schedule. Classes started at 8:30 and lasted fifty minutes. First period, Languages. Boring. Second period, Microelectronics. What? Third period, Computer Lab. Okay, cool. Fourth Period, Physical Conditioning? What! Gym! In addition to Tae Kwon Do? Get real. Definitely going to drop that one. Although I could already imagine how that conversation would play out.

Me: "Mr. Kim, I'm afraid I'm going to have to get a different class fourth period, as apparently you've forgotten that I don't do gym. Perhaps Advanced Napping would be a better option for me."

Then Mr. Kim would laugh, remind me about my agile mind, and have me enrolled in the decathlon at the next Olympics before I could blink.

Lunch was next on the schedule. I was very good at lunch. Followed by Cultures. What kind of class was that? What kind of Cultures? Then Introduction to Code Theory. Ugh. Whatever that was, it sounded boring. Seventh period was Intro to Criminal Justice. Criminal Justice? Hello? What kind of school teaches Criminal Justice to teenagers? Evading Criminal Justice, maybe.

That took us all the way to 3:30. Then there was a phrase on the schedule that sent a shiver through my body. Kitchen Duty 4–5:30 M-W-F. Kitchen Duty!

"Yep," said Pilar, "everybody has to do it. I'm on Tuesdays,

Thursdays, and Saturdays."

Her voice startled me, because I hadn't realized I'd said anything out loud.

"What is Kitchen Duty, exactly?" I asked.

"Like, stuff you do in a kitchen. Serving food. Washing dishes. Fixing stuff. Whatever Mrs. Clausen asks you to do. She runs the kitchen."

Great. Mrs. Clausen. Sounds like a pickle. I'm sure we'd be pals.

"We have the same schedule," Pilar said. "Mr. Kim told me yesterday. Hey, are you any good with computers? Because computer lab is really killing me. I just don't seem to have the aptitude for it."

"Yeah. Computers are okay. But I don't get this. What kind of class is Cultures? Or Criminal Justice?"

"Oh, man. Criminal Justice is like the coolest class ever. Mr. Quinn teaches it. He used to go to school here too. He's in his mid-twenties and works freelance for the FBI. Did I mention that he is gorgeous? Also, he's the greatest teacher. He tells all these amazing stories about criminals and investigations and crime scenes and forensics. It's awesome."

"Sounds interesting." Not.

"Oh, it is. It's my favorite class."

Great, I thought to myself. I was rooming with a Criminal Justice groupie.

"The semester started a month ago, so you'll have to catch up on some of the stuff we've covered. I can help you if you want."

"Thanks. Listen, I want to apologize for what I said yesterday. About why you're here. That was rude of me to assume—anyway, I just . . . I'm sorry."

"It's okay," she said. But she kind of blushed, like how she got here was a sensitive topic. "There are a lot of kids in here that are like you—I mean . . . not like you . . . in a bad . . . I mean with court trouble . . . sorry." She flushed.

"It's okay. That's what I was told. I just shouldn't have assumed it about you." There was an uncomfortable silence for a few minutes.

"If you don't mind my asking . . . ," she said.

I could guess. "It was either here or Juvenile Detention. I got arrested for joyriding in a stolen car. I didn't steal the car or anything; my friend had just borrowed it. But I'd had some scrapes before that, stupid stuff like vandalism and shoplifting. So this judge gave me a choice, my parents made it for me, and here I am."

"Well, today is a new day, as Mr. Kim is fond of saying. Shall we go get breakfast?"

The minute she said breakfast, my stomach growled. I hadn't realized how hungry I was. I had done more physical activity in a day at this school than I did in a month back home, and I was famished.

We headed to the cafeteria, which was somewhere in the center of the cavernous building. We were eating some fruit and cereal when Alex and Brent appeared at our table.

Alex sat down next to Pilar and kind of bumped into her with his shoulder. She giggled and bumped him back. I see. Brent sat next to me.

"Hi, guys," Pilar said. "Rachel, I think you met these guys last night, but this is Alex Scott and Brent Christian. They're roommates. I still haven't figured out how Brent puts up with this big dope." She elbowed Alex in the ribs and giggled.

They both said hi, and I said hi back. Alex reached over and took an apple slice off of Pilar's tray, and she slapped at his hand. He smiled as he ate it. It was so cute it almost made me sick. I rolled my eyes at Brent. He smirked.

I had gotten a close-up look at Alex last night in the *do jang* as he was watching me flop myself all over the place. He seemed to be a little less intense when he was out of his uniform. Brent still looked like Colin Farrell.

"So you decided to stick around?" Alex said.

"Yeah. How did you hear about that?" I said.

"I didn't. But we've all done it. It's sort of like a club," said Alex.

"Yeah. I managed to cut through the woods and find the road, but it was tough. Lucky for me, Mr. Kim caught up with me on the freeway," Brent said.

"How does he know?" I asked.

"Mr. Kim knows everything. He's got some freaky weird sixth sense, like that kid in the movie. I think he sees everything *but* the dead people," said Alex.

"Did he offer to take you to the airport?" I asked.

"He offered to drive me back to Detroit," Pilar chimed in. "Of course, he knew I had no place to go to there, but he told me at least we could get to know each other on the drive. We were about forty miles down the road before he convinced me to come back."

"He's like a wizard or something," I said.

They all agreed with me. Mr. Kim the wizard. Well, my mind was not made up yet. I had agreed to stay the month. Then we'd see.

Amazingly, the morning and early-afternoon classes kind of whizzed by. I didn't realize it until afterward, but the teachers were different than what I was used to at Beverly Hills High. For instance, I thought that first-period Languages would have me asleep in about three minutes, but the teacher, Miss Reynard, was like a language cheerleader. The class was on a Spanish section, and Miss Reynard had this very interesting way of using music to help you decode the linguistic and grammatical details when you were speaking the language. At first it was way over my head, but by the end of the period I was starting to catch on to some of it.

Then, in Microelectronics, we had to do a diagnostics exercise. A man named Mr. Sherman taught this class, and he put us at our lab stations and gave us a small circuit board that fit into a cell phone. The circuit board had a burned-out condenser or transistor or something. Then he gave us a box of old radios and telephones and calculators, probably three or four of each in the box. We had to try to find working parts on the phones and radios and get them to work in our circuit board. The only thing was, we weren't given any tools, except for a paper clip and some chewing gum. It was really weird, but I kind of got into it. Those "tools" were what you had to try to make it work.

Brent was in this class, and I noticed he was the first one to have his board repaired. He had his cell phone chirping away in a few minutes.

I didn't have a clue what to do, and Mr. Sherman spent a lot of time helping me figure it out. I couldn't imagine how a class like this would ever be useful to me, short of getting a job in a cell-phone factory. But strange as it was, the hour went by fast.

It was computer lab that blew me away. All of the machines were top of the line, with incredible operating speed and some types of software that I had never even heard of. Mrs. Pollock, this thin, kind of willowy woman, ran the lab. I tried to ignore her for a while and use my machine to get on the Internet, but the machine had no browser on it. Dang it. I had been looking forward to a whole hour of surfing, but instead we were kept busy doing an exercise on macro programs. I hadn't been able to get on the Net since I got here, and I think I was beginning to have withdrawals.

Next was the physical conditioning class, and even that went by quickly. The instructor was a sort of military-looking guy named Mr. Elliot. He looked like he'd be a real hard case, but he let me start out doing some easy stretches and walking around the track in the gymnasium, while the rest of the class did some harder stuff. I thought that was decent of him.

Then we had lunch. And it was a really good lunch. In fact, I'd never eaten in a cafeteria at any school in my life with food that good.

After lunch it was on to my Cultures class, and I was sure that here was where I would be able to catch up on my sleep. I was wrong. This teacher was Mr. Pollock, and I was taking a wild guess that he was married to Mrs. Pollock from Comp Lab. He was medium height and kind of stocky, with sandy brown hair. He had very expressive eyes and a really bright smile.

Today he was lecturing on the religious rituals of countries in South America. The way he talked made it sound like we'd be leaving for South America very soon and we'd need to make sure we knew all this stuff. And once again, I was surprised at how not boring it was. There was all kinds of weird stuff about animal gods and ritual sacrifices and other cool stuff like that.

I thought I couldn't get more excited than I had about Computer Lab, but Code Theory blew me away. It was exactly like it sounds—sort of an advanced math class where we studied how algorithms and patterns of numbers sequenced and became codes. The instructor, Mr. Chapman, was tall and thin and wore sort of geeky-looking horn-rimmed glasses, but you could tell by how he talked that he was super-smart. He told us that with the rise of the Internet and the importance of computers and computer security, a basic understanding of Code Theory was going to be essential for all of us. He explained that after graduation, we might be working with computer networks in our jobs and the Code Theory we were learning here could help us understand how to keep networks secure, and in case the network was breached, how to decipher the new code and restore the network. I could have sworn by the way he was talking that he expected us to start hacking into computer systems as soon as we left class. Why would a school teach you something like that?

Anyway, I was always good at math, and to my surprise I found the class interesting as well. They sure didn't have classes like this at my old school.

Before I knew it, it was time for Intro to Criminal Justice. Pilar and I had been together all day in the same classes, but for Intro to Criminal Justice, Alex joined us for the first time, and it was the only other class we had with Brent besides Microelectronics. We sat by them and waited for Mr. Quinn to arrive. Turned out that this class was in room 221—the very same room that I had tried to escape from. Instead of desks, we all sat in these really comfortable leather recliners. It was awesome.

Pilar was totally right about Mr. Quinn. He was young and good-looking, with a sort of blond George Clooney thing going. He was tall and he looked pretty buff. When he smiled, he had a dimple on one cheek that made his face look slightly crooked, but not in a bad way. He came over to where I sat.

"You must be our new student, Rachel Buchanan, right?" He stuck out his hand. I shook it. "Welcome aboard. I'm happy to have you here." That seemed to be the consensus of everybody at Blackthorn so far. Except for maybe Mrs. Marquardt the chatterbox. The jury was still out on her.

Mr. Quinn started his lecture, which was about the development of crime-scene analysis. The best part was about halfway through, when he killed the lights and showed a video on the big-screen TV of some techs working a crime scene. Mr. Quinn would describe how they approached the scene, broke it into a grid, and then searched each section (which they called "walking the grid") for evidence. It was way better than *CSI*. Again the hour was over quickly. I didn't even realize he'd been talking for a whole fifty minutes, because he was kind of mesmerizing.

The only thing that was really boring during the whole day was Kitchen Duty. I'm totally helpless in a kitchen. At home our maid, Rosa, does all the cooking and housekeeping. God knows Cynthia never cooked, and I never really learned how to do much beyond pour cereal. Mrs. Clausen was totally unlike the cafeteria lady who ran the Beverly Hills High cafeteria back home. She was a small woman with a loud voice, and she spoke in a very thick German accent. The food she put out, I have to say, was a lot better than what we had back home. There was a lot of fresh stuff, like fruits and vegetables, and nothing that came out of a box. Okay. One more mark in Blackthorn's favor: good food.

That evening, after Kitchen Duty and dinner, I was back in the *do jang* for Tae Kwon Do. Mr. Torres, the other Tae Kwon Do master they had told me about, taught the class. He was about six feet two with black hair and green eyes. When we got there he was doing handstand push-ups, and he did twenty of them, which I know because I counted. I was impressed. He seemed nice enough, but he also gave off the impression that he was a no-nonsense kind of guy. There would be no karaoke nights in the *do jang* while Mr. Torres was in charge. After calisthenics, he put me off to the side with Alex to work on my first pattern some more. I could remember all of the words of the sound-off, but I was still pretty hopeless with the movements. Alex laughed at me only a couple of times that night.

The next day and the day after were pretty much the same. I had to admit that as much as I didn't want them to be, the classes were pretty interesting. Even Physical Conditioning. Mr. Elliot came up with a lot of cool exercises and games that seemed to make the hour go by fast, yet you still felt like you'd done something. I still didn't like the Kitchen Duty so much, but Mrs. Clausen was a sweet little lady and it was hard not to like her. She was patient and explained everything and was really hands-on about teaching you stuff about food.

By the end of the first week I even managed to get through the movements of the first pattern of Tae Kwon Do with only two mistakes and falling down only once. But Alex was still an arrogant jerk in the *do jang,* as far as I was concerned. No matter how much he drilled me on the techniques, I just couldn't pick it up fast enough.

There was this one technique called *chwa dwi chagi,* which is Korean for left backward kick. It should have been easy for me since I'm left-handed, but for some reason it got all confused in my mind, and each time Alex gave the command I would kick back with my right foot instead.

"No, Rachel, the left foot," he said after I'd done it wrong again.

"I'm trying, Alex, give me a break," I said. I stopped a moment to mop the sweat off my forehead. All I seemed to do at this stupid school was sweat.

"It's Mr. Scott in the *do jang,* not Alex," he said.

"Yeah, whatever," I said. He hated my laxity with the manners in the *do jang,* so of course my only option was to be even more lax. Loser.

"Someday, when I'm fourth Dan, you'll have to call me Master Scott," he said. He was trying to goad me, and it was working.

"The day I call you master is the day Eminem joins the Backstreet Boys," I said.

"*Do jang* rules," he said.

"Yeah, well, don't hold your breath," I said. "I'll be long gone from this place before that ever happens." I took my stance again because Mr. Kim had come into the *do jang* and was watching us, but when Alex gave the command, I messed it up again and kicked back with my right foot. Alex just shook his head.

So I couldn't say that the Tae Kwon Do lessons were going along so well.

Still, the weeks went by fast. So fast that I almost forgot about the red door and the Top Floor wing. But one day during physical conditioning, we went outside to do some work on a rock-climbing wall that was part of the athletic fields. When we came back in, we went down the same corridor and past the hallway that led to the red door.

"Hey, Pilar, what is the Top Floor wing, anyway?" I asked.

"It's a special wing for students that have special abilities," she said. That's not an answer. That is being Mr. Kim's little parrot.

"I know that; that's what Mr. Kim told me. But what is it? Who gets to be part of it?"

"It's mostly students in the final year of classes here. If

you're good at something like Code Theory or Languages, you can take the Top Floor-level courses. It's a lot tougher and stricter. You sometimes get to go to special assignments or classes off site. But it's all pretty secret."

"Why the hush-hush?"

"I don't know. Mr. Kim just wants everybody to concentrate on their work and not worry about other stuff, I guess."

"How come nobody else can go up there except them?"

"I don't know. It's just Mr. Kim's rule. Nobody questions it," she said.

Nobody questions his rules, huh? We'll see about that.

The next day we were out on the climbing wall again and I was having my usual klutzy time of it. I did okay going up, though it took me longer than anybody else. Today, instead of being lowered back down on the safety rope like before, Mr. Elliot wanted me to try rappelling back down on the rope. This is much harder than it looks, and as I got about two-thirds of the way down, my leg got tangled up in the rope and I twisted upside down and fell the rest of the way, landing in a heap.

One of the girls in the class apparently thought this was quite funny, because she started laughing. I didn't know what her name was, but she was one of those disgustingly athletic people who never fall off rock-climbing walls.

I jumped to my feet and got right in her grille.

"What's so funny?" I said. Loudly. The rest of the class went quiet.

"You. You can't do anything right, and the rest of us have to spend all of our class time waiting for you to not be a spaz. Why don't you get in shape?" I think her name was Melinda or Miranda or something like that. Time to teach her a lesson. I may be from Beverly Hills, but nobody laughs at me.

"Why don't you shut your mouth!"

"Why don't you make me!" she said. I'd seen this girl in Tae Kwon Do and I knew she could probably kick my butt. But I was mad. The world started to turn red, and I could feel my heart start pounding in my chest. I was sick of this school. Sick of being made to do all of this stuff that I couldn't do and didn't understand. Then to be laughed at? That was the end of it.

I reached out and pushed Melinda/Miranda/Whoever she was in the chest and she stumbled over a pile of rope and sat down. But she came up hard and fast, and the next thing I knew I was on my back and she was sitting on my chest holding me down. She was about to punch me in the jaw when Mr. Elliot grabbed her from behind and pulled her off me.

"Enough!" he shouted. "What the heck is going on here?"

Missy or Melissa or Meredith smirked at me and said, "Nothing."

"You know the rules. No fighting," he said.

"She started it." Could I *be* any more lame? She started it?

"Rachel, enough. I don't care who started it. Marissa, hit the track and give me two laps. Rachel, you hit the showers and get ready for your next class."

"But—" I started to say. But Mr. Elliot just shook his head and pointed toward the school.

I unhooked my harness. I could hear Marissa and a couple of her friends laughing as she walked through them to head out to the track. I looked at Pilar before I left, and she kind of shrugged her shoulders and looked down at the ground sheepishly. I didn't know what the rules were about fighting among students at Blackthorn Academy, but I'd go out on a limb and say they were probably against it.

I stormed across the athletic field, slammed my way through the door, and rounded the corner that led to the locker rooms. Sixth-sense Mr. Kim was waiting in the hall. He smiled and asked me to take a walk with him.

As we walked, Mr. Kim spoke.

"Would you like to tell me what happened between you and Marissa?"

"You were watching?" I said.

He nodded. Man, he floated around this school like a ghost. Didn't he ever have actual work to do? Reports to write, forms to fill out and stuff? It seemed like all he had done in the weeks I'd been here was keep an eye on me.

"I'd rather not talk about it," I said.

"Very well. Perhaps when you are ready to discuss it. If I may, though, I would suggest that in the future, when you are confronted with ridicule, you choose an option other than fighting one of my best Tae Kwon Do students."

"Well, if your best students learn to shut their pie holes, that won't be a problem." Again, here he was, telling me what to think and feel. I didn't think I could take another second of this place!

As usual, Mr. Kim abruptly changed the subject.

"So Rachel, it's been two weeks. I just wanted to check in

with you and have a discussion about how things are going. If you'll indulge me for a moment, there is something I want to show you first." Like I had a choice.

We walked back out to the atrium of the school. Off to one side of the atrium was a big glass case with all kinds of trophies, plaques, and different photos of Blackthorn students. Mr. Kim stopped in front of the case. He motioned me to stand next to him.

"Take a look at some of these photos, Rachel," Mr. Kim said.

Boring. I'll bet he was getting ready to go all *Good Will Hunting* on me and give me some big life lesson speech about my special abilities again. Snore. But he was in charge, so I looked at the stupid trophies and photographs. Some of them were of individual students in athletic uniforms from the school. Some were photographs of teams. Some of the trophies were for sports, some for things like math and science competitions. Some of them had little guys in Tae Kwon Do poses on top. Some of them looked like they'd been there for a long time. I was not impressed.

"Do you see anyone you recognize?" he asked.

I looked over the faces in the photos again. At first I didn't see anyone I knew, but then I spotted a face I'd seen before—Judge Kerrigan. Only, in this picture she looked like she was about fifteen. Her hair was long and wavy and wasn't done up in an unfashionable bun like she wore it now. Still pretty bad hair, though. She was wearing a field hockey uniform and holding a trophy. I pointed at the photo and looked at Mr. Kim.

"Judge Kerrigan?"

"Yes. Judge Theresa Kerrigan, Blackthorn Academy class of 1984. She was a star forward on the Academy field hockey team. But only after she decided to stay at the school, of course. That took some convincing on my part."

"Field hockey, huh? I can see her using a stick to hit things," I cracked.

Mr. Kim smiled. He pointed to another photo of a man in a suit handing a plaque to a younger man. The younger man was Mr. Quinn, the Criminology teacher.

"That is Mr. Quinn, at the age of sixteen, receiving an Award of Appreciation from the Director of the FBI."

"Yeah, right. You're kidding me."

"Mr. Quinn is, as one might say, a computer genius—in addition to having a Ph.D. in abnormal psychology. When he was a student here, he spent all of his free time in the computer lab. Remember that computers and databases were not as advanced in the late 1980s as they are now. Mr. Quinn developed a program that helped the FBI catalog criminal cases from jurisdictions around the country based on common characteristics of the crime. Cataloging the information was easy. Making it usable was the hard part. That was Mr. Quinn's breakthrough. It was an early model of their system, and it became the foundation of the FBI's National Crime Index database that they use today."

I consider myself something of a computer geek, so I knew Mr. Kim was talking about the NCIC database. You saw it on TV and in movies all the time. The cops in those shows were always running names through "NCIC" to see if anyone had a criminal record.

"He did that while he was here? As a student?" Okay, that's impressive.

Mr. Kim nodded. "And look here," he said, pointing to three boys dressed in Blackthorn Academy basketball uniforms. They all looked identical to one another. "Those are Mrs. Clausen's sons. Triplets. Mrs. Clausen's husband died when the boys were ten years old. She took a job here and brought her boys with her. They all graduated ten years ago. Two of them are in the military, and the third is a police detective in Miami. Mrs. Clausen, luckily for us, stayed on after they left.

"All of the students who have come to Blackthorn Academy are special to me, Rachel. All of them have become more than students; they are my family. I know that it was not your choice to come here. But in this short time, watching you and getting to know you somewhat, I've become very fond of you. So have your teachers. They tell me that they sense greatness in you. Especially Mr. Quinn. He has been amazed by the questions you have asked in class. He thinks you have a real aptitude for criminology."

He does? I thought to myself. Funny—I'd been so busy listening, I hadn't realized I'd even asked any questions. Mr. Quinn thought I was amazing? Shut up!

"What I am saying, Rachel, is that I hope you will choose to stay when the month is up. But I want to make sure you realize that I will honor our agreement. If you wish to return to California, I will make arrangements for you to do so. However,

I hope that will not be the case. I think you would prosper here. Have you thought about your decision yet?"

Well, the truth was that up until this morning and my tussle with that witch Marissa, I hadn't. I had meant to. When Mr. Kim brought me back to the school that night, I had expected that I'd drag myself through the month and then jump on a plane back to BH. That was totally my plan. But then I started classes, and the first two weeks had gone by so fast, I hadn't really thought about that part of my plan at all. So now I was caught a little off guard. Darn that Mr. Kim.

"Well, I don't know. There is still a lot of stuff I don't like about this place. I don't like the Tae Kwon Do. Mrs. Clausen is really nice, but I'm helpless in the kitchen. And I can't get on the Internet. I like the Internet."

Mr. Kim smiled but didn't say anything.

I decided to see how far I could go.

"I don't feel like I'm cut out for this place. You have to do all this studying and gym, and I'm a total klutz. If I stay I don't want to do any of that stuff."

Mr. Kim smiled and raised his eyebrows as if waiting for me to continue.

"I don't fit in here, Mr. Kim. I mean, I'm sure for brainiacs like Pilar and jocks like Alex, it's fine. But I'm not like them."

"I see," said Mr. Kim. "Unfortunately, your options are somewhat limited. If you leave, you will most likely end up in Juvenile Detention."

"I know!" I shouted. "I know that. Okay? I know that I don't have any options, I know that this place is probably better than

Juvie, but I still don't like it here!"

"Rachel. Please. Calm down. Let me help you. Trust me, this will work out and you will grow to like it here. I promise."

"How can you promise me something like that? You don't even listen to me when I tell you I can't do this stuff. What makes you think I'll ever like it here? What gives you the right to think you can control my life like that? You go on and on about how special I am and my agile mind and all that garbage. I've only been here two weeks. You don't even know me."

"Rachel. You misunderstand. All the things that I have told you about yourself and how the others here see you are true. What I tell you I observe about your mind and your intelligence is what I believe. In fact, I am beginning to believe there is something very unique about you. And I know that, given time, you'll adjust quite readily to your life here. But you must follow the rules and you must meet us halfway. Without that . . . " He didn't finish.

Yeah, well, rules this and responsibilities that, and blah, blah, blah, blah, blah.

I didn't know what to say. I had a feeling that I could argue with Mr. Kim forever and all he would do is smile and nod and make a little Zen speech to me about mastering my rage before my rage becomes my master. Maybe that was his style. He just kept after people until he wore you down.

"Give me one good reason why I should stay here," I said.

"Because, deep down, you really don't want to leave."

Whoa. What was he doing now? Joking with me? Like I couldn't wait to see Blackthorn Academy in my rearview mirror. *Adios, amigo.* Catch you on the flip-flop. If you see me getting smaller, it's because I'm walking away. There was no way I wanted to stay here. He was crazy.

"What makes you think that?"

"Because you are intrigued by this place. It has piqued your curiosity. It is a puzzle that you have not yet figured out. And because you want to find out if you are tough enough to make it through a year here."

With that, Mr. Kim turned and walked away and left me standing alone with my thoughts.

PART TWO

CHAPTER TEN

Thinks He's So Smart

I'm not stupid. I know he was trying to psyche me out. Telling me I may not be "tough enough" to make it through a year so I'd get mad at him and stay just to prove him wrong. Like those cheap reverse-psychology tricks could work on me. He's not as smart as he thinks. Or else he doesn't know anything about teenagers.

I stood there for quite a while after he left, thinking. I don't know how long. I was aware of people coming and going through the atrium, but nobody paid any attention to me. What was really bugging me is that he was right. If I really thought about it, what other options did I have?

Charles and Cynthia didn't want me. They may have thought it was neat to have a kid when I was little. But to them a teenager was nothing more than an annoyance. I didn't have any close friends or relatives I could turn to, now that Gramps was dead. Jamie and Grego were fun to hang with, and I guess Jamie and I were pretty good girlfriends, but in the end, look at the evidence. They left me hanging that night in the car. They took off as soon as they had the chance. Same with Boozer. But with Boozer, I knew up front he couldn't be counted on. It wasn't like I had any expectations of him.

The plain fact, and Mr. Kim had somehow figured it out the moment he'd laid eyes on me, was that I really was alone. I had no place to go. This Academy was it for me. I could go back to L.A. and try to hide out, but they'd catch up to me eventually. Even if I crashed at Boozer's, he'd end up blabbing to someone and eventually I'd get busted. And the living-on-the-street option was not so appealing. Besides, there was no Internet access on the street either.

But the thought of staying at this school was just weighing me down. I didn't see any way I could last a year here. I'd have to give it the rest of the month and think of something else. Mr. Kim had promised me he'd let me go and not tell the judge. I'd figure out something then. Once my month was up, I could leave. Okay. I could do this. I was still me. I could treat it like the army or something. Just get through the next two weeks and then I'm back to me. No problem. Really.

And then all of a sudden it was two weeks later. My one-month "probation" was up. It seemed like it had rocketed by. Except for Kitchen Duty. And Tae Kwon Do. But a funny thing there. After three weeks of taking classes every day, Mr. Kim had me test for my ninth gup. That's the first rank in TKD. I thought he was crazy, but I got through the first pattern without any mistakes. To my great surprise, I passed the test. At the belt ceremony Mr. Kim put a piece of yellow tape around the end of my belt. He smiled and bowed and looked at me like I'd just won an Oscar or something, and the whole class applauded. (Well, technically they applauded for everybody who moved up in rank, but it was still cool.) He told me that in another month, if I took class every day and worked hard, I could test for eighth gup, and if I passed I'd get a yellow belt.

After that first hurdle, I started not minding Tae Kwon Do class so much. It kind of started to get interesting. For one thing, after the first week, I wasn't so sore after class. And Mr. Kim started to tell all kinds of cool stories about how Tae Kwon Do was invented by Buddhist monks to give the Korean peasants something to fight back with every time the Japanese Samurai would invade Korea. All of a sudden, these peasants learned Tae Kwon Do and started kicking the snot out of these Samurai invaders and the Japanese didn't know what to do about it. I love stories about that kind of stuff. I still had problems with some of the more advanced movements, like that stupid *chwa dwi chagi* move, but I was making progress.

Still, I felt restless and I was looking forward to my month being up. I was sure I didn't belong here, even if I hadn't heard a word from Charles and Cynthia. No surprise there: out of sight, out of mind.

Part of the reason I felt so weird about the place was Pilar. I mean, we seemed to get along okay and we had worked our way into this kind of truce. But there was something that wasn't right about that girl. She kept staring at me all the time. Most of the time it was like if she stared at me long enough, she'd be able to figure me out. Then sometimes I'd catch her looking at me and she'd have a frown on her face as if I was about to break something. I'd stare back at her then, and she'd look away and act all embarrassed like I'd caught her up to something. It was almost like she was spying on me. It was a little unsettling.

Add to that the fact that she talked in her sleep a lot. She would mumble words and phrases that made no sense. She'd wake me up in the middle of the night with all the talking in her sleep. The next morning I'd ask her about her dreams and she'd say she didn't remember, but I knew she did. She just didn't want to tell me.

And it wasn't just Pilar, either. Mr. Kim always seemed to be keeping pretty close tabs on me. Maybe it was just my imagination, but it seemed like I would be walking to class or in the cafeteria or somewhere and I'd glance up and he'd be there watching me. A few times he asked me about the dream I'd had in the woods. Did I ever have the same dream again? Did I have any ideas about what the dream might have meant? He always made it sound like he was just interested in people's dreams and he would tell me about strange dreams he had, but I still found it all a little weird.

One good thing was after those first weeks I finally could find my way around the Academy better. It was a big place and there was still a lot of the Academy that I hadn't explored. In fact, it seemed like the school was a lot bigger than it needed to be for the couple hundred students that were there. But each day was busy, and I really didn't think about things all that much. I was just looking forward to my month being up so I could get out of here. Then that day finally arrived.

And all hell broke loose.

CHAPTER ELEVEN

Now You See Him

The morning that Mr. Kim disappeared was the day after we went on a class trip into Washington, D.C. We'd been to see a special exhibit at the Randall Gallery, which was a gallery that specialized in antiquities and rare manuscripts. In our Cultures class we were studying medieval societies, and we were on a section of our text that dealt with literature about the Crusades. I never thought the words "Medieval" and "Literature" would ever be anywhere near a conversation that had anything to do with me, but Mr. Pollock made the class so interesting. He wanted us to go to the gallery to see several actual books and manuscripts that had come from that period.

If this had been BH High, I would have cut the field trip and gone to the mall, especially since it was on a Sunday. But Mr.

Pollock told us all kinds of cool stories about the stuff we were going to see, like that these manuscripts told the stories of Crusaders from both sides of the Holy Wars. They told about the exploits of the English kings and Muslim potentates who fought battles for dozens of years in the Middle East.

Mr. Pollock was all excited because part of the exhibit was something called the *Book of Seraphim,* which told the story of the Emperor Flavius, who ruled Rome in the last days of the Roman Empire. It was first discovered in what is now the country of Kuzbekistan during the Middle Ages. Apparently the *Book of Seraphim* was more than two thousand years old, and King Richard III had spent many years trying to capture it during the Crusades, because the Muslims believed that whoever possessed it would have mystical powers. Nobody knows why they thought that. Supposedly Flavius had written down stuff that was supposed to give armies great power. King Richard III thought if he had it, the Muslims might give up and surrender, but he could never get his hands on it. Then it was apparently lost for several centuries, until just a few years ago. Now the government of Kuzbekistan was letting it tour museums around the world, and it was a really big deal to get to see it. When Mr. Pollock talked about this stuff, he got all excited and sort of bounced around the room telling us the stories. You practically forgot that you were learning about some dusty old book.

The next day, on our way in from yet more rock climbing (apparently Mr. Elliot felt that all of us would be climbing Mt. Everest someday), we passed the corridor that led to the Top

Floor. Mr. Kim was in the hallway talking to these two guys in suits. They were having an animated conversation, and Mr. Kim was pacing back and forth. One of the guys seemed familiar to me somehow, but I didn't know why. He was taking notes in a notebook as they talked. It seemed to me that Mr. Kim was a little excited or upset (it was hard to tell with Mr. Kim), because it looked like the two men were trying to calm him down.

It looked weird. Since they hadn't noticed me yet and I'm incurably nosy, I bent down and pretended to be tying my shoe while the rest of the class filed in from outside. This enabled me to do what every smart and conscientious teenager would do: eavesdrop on their conversation. Unfortunately, I could only make out two words: One sounded like "Misses" and then I clearly heard Mr. Kim say "Seraphim." Then Mr. Kim motioned for the men to follow him. He took a key from his pocket and unlocked the door to the Top Floor wing. The guy who was taking notes shut his little notebook, and as he moved forward a piece of paper fell out of it. All three men disappeared inside the door.

Now, hold on just a minute! We full-time students can't go to the Top Floor, and it's all secret-secret, but a couple of suits show up and Mr. Kim takes them right on in? How fair is that? Not very.

Well, my curiosity was killing me. I know it's wrong to pry into other people's business, but I just can't help myself. It's my worst vice. I snuck over and picked up the piece of paper—only it wasn't paper, it was a business card. It said SPECIAL AGENT NATHAN TYLER, FEDERAL BUREAU OF INVESTIGATION and it had the FBI seal on it.

Strange. What was an FBI agent talking to Mr. Kim about? And even stranger, why did an FBI agent seem so familiar to me? The FBI had never busted me, so that couldn't be it. Still, I could swear I'd seen him somewhere before. I didn't have a lot of time right then to think about it, because the rest of the class was almost out of sight already. I stuffed the card in the pocket of my shorts and moved on to my next class.

But all day long it drove me nuts. Mr. Kim was talking to some FBI agents and I had very clearly heard him say "Seraphim." This on the day after we had gone to see the *Book of Seraphim* at a nearby museum. Plus, he had taken them into the Top Floor wing. And I could swear that that FBI agent was familiar, and that was really bugging me.

I didn't see Mr. Kim for the rest of the afternoon. That was highly unusual, since he was always a visible presence around the school. He usually came into the lunchroom to talk and eat with students, and you would see him in the hallways between classes a lot. But for the rest of that day he was nowhere to be seen. I hoped he showed up soon, because I wanted to meet with him so we could arrange to get me out of here.

By the time Kitchen Duty rolled around, I couldn't take it anymore. All the strange feelings I had about this place seemed to crystallize: (1) The classes were weird. Code Theory? Criminal Justice? (2) My roommate stared at me all the time and talked in her sleep. (3) How had Mr. Kim known so much about me when I got here? I mean, he knew *everything*. And then (4) there was this separate floor of the school that apparently no one but "special" students and FBI agents was allowed to see. It was all just too weird. There had to be a explanation. So I hatched a plan.

It wasn't a very good plan. Kind of lame, actually. My plan was to sneak into Mr. Kim's office and see if he had some kind of files I could check out. Not for the other students—I'd only look at my own file, not anyone else's. If I could find it and read it, maybe it would tell me how he'd known all about me. Maybe it was the FBI that had checked up on me before I came here and that was how I recognized that guy. Maybe he had been sent to California to check me out and I had spotted him somehow.

I knew it wasn't much, but it was a place to start. Mr. Kim was hardly ever in his office, so I figured it would be easy to get in. Making sure I didn't get caught would be the hard part. But I had a Plan B. Since it was one month to the day since I'd come to the school, Mr. Kim and I needed to have our little "chat" about my future. If I got caught in his office, I'd just say I was looking for him so we could have our discussion.

I mean, as far as I was concerned, I was already on my way out of this school. I still didn't have a plan once I got to California. But now all this strange stuff happening had made me curious and I didn't like the idea of leaving with a mystery unsolved.

I had about thirty minutes before I had to be in the kitchen, so I headed to the corridor that led down to Mr. Kim's office. I peered around the corner and made sure there was no one there. So far, so good. I crept quietly down the hallway and listened in front of Mr. Kim's door, but couldn't hear any noise coming from inside. I reached out and started to turn the knob, but just as I was about to open it, the door directly across the hallway flew open. Mrs. Marquardt stood there staring at me. She startled me so much that I almost screamed. How did she know I was there? She must be a witch.

She gave me a curious look.

"Rachel, what are you doing?" she asked. Probably the most words I'd ever heard Mrs. Marquardt say in a row.

"Hi, Mrs. Marquardt. How are you today?" I tried to keep that "I'm up to something" tone out of my voice.

"Fine. What are you doing here?" Her intense gaze was a little intimidating.

"Oh, I was just on my way to Kitchen Duty and I forgot something in my room."

"This isn't the way to your room." I noticed for the first time that Mrs. Marquardt had a very long nose, and right then she was looking down it at me. I could also tell that since she had caught me with my hand on the doorknob to Mr. Kim's office, I had just screwed up and told a very bad lie. *Come on, Rachel. Get in the game.*

"I know that. I was just daydreaming and turned the wrong way. I still get lost around here a lot. But since I was here any-way, I thought I'd check and see if Mr. Kim was available. We were supposed to meet today." I kind of shrugged my shoulders and sighed. Poor little lost Rachel Buchanan. So far from home. Mrs. Marquardt's expression didn't change, so I let out another big, sad-sounding sigh. Nothing. She was a tough one.

"Mr. Kim is quite busy. In the future, make an appointment.

Now you'd better get going. Work period starts soon."

Mrs. Marquardt dismissed me and went back into her office. Before she shut the door she turned around and stared at me again, like she wanted to make sure I wasn't going to hang around. "Make an appointment"? I'd make an appointment all right. How dare she? I waved and started back down the hall. Just then I heard Mr. Kim's door open and looked back to see Mr. Kim and the two men he'd been talking to come out of his office. The two agents nodded at Mrs. Marquardt and turned to walk the opposite way down the hallway. Mr. Kim didn't say anything; he just went back into his office and closed the door. I felt my knees turn to jelly. I had almost walked in on them! That was close. Would have been fun trying to explain that one. Thank goodness Mrs. Marquardt had caught me.

As Mrs. Marquardt turned to watch them head toward the atrium, I ducked quickly into a nearby doorway and waited. I could hear their footsteps getting farther away. Then I heard Mrs. Marquardt's office door close. I peeked. No one in the hallway.

This whole thing was just out-of-control bizarre. Mr. Kim had clearly been upset this morning. And now it looked like the agents had been here the entire day talking to Mr. Kim. Something was going on. As Boozer, a great fan of Spider-Man, would say, "my spider-sense was tingling."

I figured I had nothing to lose by confronting Mr. Kim directly and asking him what the heck was going on. I knew he probably wouldn't tell me anything, but I could be persistent and annoying, and I might be able to wear him down until he spilled the beans.

I walked quietly back down the hall to Mr. Kim's office. I could hear a radio playing softly in Mrs. Marquardt's office, and the soft *click-click* of her keyboard. I knocked on Mr. Kim's door. No answer. Maybe he couldn't hear me. So I knocked a little louder, but not so loud that Mrs. Marquardt would hear me. Still no answer.

Okay. I could do the smart thing here and go back to my room and forget the whole episode. That would work. Just forget the whole thing.

I tried the knob. Like everything else at the Academy, the door wasn't locked. Very trusting souls, these Blackthorn Academy residents. I knocked lightly as I opened the door.

"Mr. Kim? Hello?"

I swung the door open all the way and found the office empty. No Mr. Kim. Strange. I had only had my back to the office for a few seconds, and I was sure he couldn't have left without me seeing him. So where did he go? I closed the door and crossed the office to his desk. Maybe he was hiding. Right. A game of hide-and-seek. I walked around the desk and looked under it. No Mr. Kim. The windows were shut and the blinds were down, so I didn't think he could have left by the window. But just to be sure, I pulled open one of the blinds and looked out the window that was directly behind Mr. Kim's desk. No rope or bedsheet hanging down to the ground. No Mr. Kim anywhere in sight.

So had he disappeared? Did he have some kind of secret ninja invisibility mojo he was using? Had he actually been standing in the corner, but I couldn't see him?

"Mr. Kim? Are you here?"

No answer.

I noticed a pad of paper on his desk. When I'd been in his office a few weeks before, his desktop had been completely clear; no pens or anything. Now there was a pad of paper on the desk, with a single word written on it: "MITHRAS." Was that what I'd heard him say in the hallway when he was talking to the suits? I'd thought he said "Mrs." or "misses." What the heck was MITHRAS? And yet it sounded oddly like something I'd heard before somewhere else. There was something out there, in a thread of memory that I couldn't quite place. Mithras.

Since I was snooping anyway, I decided to look in a desk drawer. Maybe just one. But to my surprise, all of the desk drawers were empty. No pens or paper or paper clips or Scotch tape or markers or staples or stamps or anything. Completely empty. Apparently Mr. Kim was not a fan of office supplies. All of a sudden, I noticed the knob on the door start to turn. Whoa! I'd be in so much trouble if I were caught in here. I quickly ducked underneath the desk.

I couldn't see who was coming in, but I could hear Mrs. Marquardt's radio from across the hall. She must have left her door open and come into Mr. Kim's office for something. Then I heard a gasp. Definitely Mrs. Marquardt. For a minute I thought I was busted. I tried to move my head a little bit to look up at the window behind Mr. Kim's desk where I could see Mrs. Marquardt's reflection. I saw her reach down and tear the top sheet of paper off the pad on Mr. Kim's desk. She looked upset.

I realized then that she didn't know I was there. She gasped again, and then I heard her crumple the paper. Her reflection moved away and then I heard the office door close, followed a few seconds later by the sound of Mrs. Marquardt's office door closing. Safe.

What the heck was going on? That was a really strange display from Mrs. Marquardt. Or, okay, this might be normal behavior for Mrs. Marquardt, for all I knew. But Mr. Kim had definitely vanished from a closed room. Then Mrs. Marquardt blanched when she saw the word "MITHRAS" on a sheet of paper. And two strange FBI guys in suits were the last people I'd seen talking to Mr. Kim. Maybe, while my back was turned, they offed him and stuffed his body in a file cabinet. I'd better check those file cabinets in the corner. One of them could be holding Mr. Kim's body!

Hmm, on second thought, maybe I'd let someone else check those. *Sorry, Mr. Kim, I truly hope you're not dead, but Rachel doesn't do the "find the dead body" thing.* Besides, he was about a million-degree black belt in Tae Kwon Do. I doubted two guys like that could take him without shooting him or something. So he was almost certainly still alive, just gone. But where?

I needed time to think about this. I was going to be late for Kitchen Duty if I didn't hustle. I'd probably just missed Mr. Kim leaving his office. He'd just skipped out without my knowing. That had to be it. You can't just disappear from a closed room.

I crossed to the door and opened it a crack. Mrs. Marquardt's door was closed, so I stepped quietly into the hall.

Okay, I knew this was crazy, but I wanted to see if those guys were still in the atrium or out in front of the school. If I got a closer look at them, maybe I could figure out where I'd seen that one guy before.

I started down the hall to the atrium, thinking what a strange day this had been. Mr. Kim acting more worked up than I'd ever seen him. Mrs. Marquardt acting like she'd seen a ghost. And what the heck was MITHRAS? But Kitchen Duty was in fifteen minutes, and I needed to haul butt if I was going to be on time. I would have made it too—if I hadn't rounded the corner and run square into Special Agent Nathan Tyler of the FBI.

CHAPTER TWELVE

Rachel, You've Got a Lot of Explaining to Do

"Oops. Sorry," I said. He was the guy that looked familiar somehow. I started to go around him, trying to act casual. But his voice stopped me.

"What are you doing here?" he asked.

I thought about answering "growing older." But he kind of had a cop attitude and instinct told me not to crack wise. Maybe he didn't realize that he was the one out of place here.

"Going to the kitchen," I said.

"The kitchen is on the other side of the building," he said. How did he know that?

"Well, duh. I know that. I'm on my way to the atrium. It's my turn to dust the trophy cases this week." That was an incredibly good lie, and I was really proud of myself for thinking of it so fast.

The guy just looked at me for a minute.

"I thought you said you were going to the kitchen," he said. Oops.

"I meant I'm going to the kitchen *after* I dust the trophy cases." Whew.

He squinted at me.

"Didn't I see you in this hallway a few minutes ago?"

"I'm sorry, may I ask who you are? You're not a teacher, are you? I've only been here a short while and I don't know everyone, but you don't look familiar." Another lie. I stared back at him. He didn't say anything, so I went on, "You know, we're not supposed to have strangers lurking around the school. Maybe I should call Mr. Kim and report you." That ought to fix him. You can't push Rachel Buchanan around!

He reached into his suit and pulled out a badge case. He flipped it open and showed me his official FBI badge and ID.

"My name's Tyler, Nathan. I'm a Special Agent for the FBI. My partner and I were leaving, and I forgot something I wanted to ask Mr. Kim. Now answer my question. Didn't I see you in the hallway a few minutes ago?"

"Is Tyler your first name or your last? Because you've got one of those names that could go either way. Tyler Nathan or Nathan Tyler. Me, I can't do that, my last name's Buchanan. Buchanan Rachel doesn't make sense. I always wanted one of those two-way names just to shake things up." I was stalling. Agent Tyler was staring at me. I didn't know what was going on yet, but until I did, I wasn't going to sing to the Feds. Then, as luck would have it, Mrs. Marquardt came around the corner.

"May I help you, Agent Tyler?" she asked. She strolled down the hall to where we stood.

"I just had another question for Mr. Kim," Tyler said.

"I'm sorry, he is no longer in his office. In fact, I don't know where he is. I can have him call you when he comes in."

"Sure. Okay. Umm. All right, that'll be fine." For some reason he was acting nervous, like he wanted to say something but didn't want to say it in front of me.

Finally Agent Tyler gave me another look, then turned and left. Where had I seen him before? It was driving me nuts.

I was watching him walk down the hall and darn near jumped out of my skin when I felt Mrs. Marquardt's hand on my shoulder.

"Rachel, what are you doing here? This isn't the way to the kitchen."

Mrs. Marquardt was turning into quite the chatterbox.

"I know. I was on my way, then I heard a noise down here." (Oh, how lame. I heard a noise? But it was all I could think of.) "I was just checking it out and then that agent guy came up. What's up with that? Why is an FBI agent talking to Mr. Kim?"

"Go to Kitchen Duty, Rachel."

"What?" When you're being asked to do something you don't want to do, I've often found it very useful to fake hearing loss.

"Kitchen Duty. Now."

That Mrs. Marquardt. She could be a real cutup when she wanted to be.

All the way to the kitchen, I kept thinking about three things: Where did Mr. Kim go? What was Mithras and where had I heard it? And where had I seen that Agent Tyler before? I hadn't been anywhere but the Academy for the last four weeks, except for the class trip to D.C., and the more I thought about it, I doubted I'd seen him in California after my unfortunate misunderstanding with the police. If the FBI were going to send someone to check me out, they would have used someone from one of the offices out there, right? But I know I'd seen him somewhere.

I was more convinced than ever that something about this school was just not right. If this place was supposed to be a school for kids with problems, why weren't they teaching normal classes? I mean, why not science and geography instead of Code Theory and Criminology? And why the emphasis on martial arts? It was all just too bizarre.

Not to mention this mysterious Top Floor. Well, that was enough for me. After Kitchen Duty today I was heading back to Mr. Kim's office and we were going to have a little chat about all this. I was going to get some answers. Okay, probably not. But I was sure going to ask numerous questions. Besides, today was the day I'd completed my month, and I meant to hold him to his promise to get me out of here.

I got to the kitchen with about thirty seconds to spare, and for the first time since I'd been at Blackthorn, the time dragged. I couldn't concentrate, and Mrs. Clausen kept asking me if I was feeling all right. After my shift was over, I grabbed a tray of food and headed out to the tables to find Pilar. I was dying to tell someone about all of this stuff, and she seemed like my only logical candidate. Despite the night murmurs and the staring at me all the time, she seemed pretty smart. She'd been here longer than me and maybe she'd have some ideas.

I told her what I'd seen. I could tell she didn't believe me when I said the part about Mr. Kim disappearing from his office. But she admitted the other stuff was weird.

Then it hit me. I suddenly knew where I'd seen Agent Tyler before.

"That's it," I said out loud.

"What's it?" asked Pilar.

"I know where I saw that Agent Tyler before," I said.

"Where?"

"Here!"

"In the lunchroom?"

"No. Here at Blackthorn. He used to be a student here. I'm sure of it." I looked at my watch and saw that there was twenty minutes left in the dinner period. I grabbed Pilar's arm.

"Come on. I've got to show you this."

Pilar protested but didn't put up much of a fight. I led her from the cafeteria all the way across the building and back to the atrium. When we got there, I raced over to the trophy case where Mr. Kim had shown me the Blackthorn highlights a few weeks before. I searched through all of the photos, looking at the faces. There he was. Nathan Tyler, co-captain of the Blackthorn Academy basketball team from the year 1990.

"Aha!" I said, and pointed. Pilar looked at the picture.

"How do you know it's the same guy?"

"It's him. There's no doubt. A little older now, but he still looks the same. Besides, the caption says 'Nathan Tyler, Co-Captain.' It's totally him. So why was he talking to Mr. Kim?"

"Maybe he was just coming back to visit," she said. "Maybe he and Mr. Kim have kept in touch and he was in the area, so he dropped by to say hello."

Sweet, reasonable, non-conspiracy-believing Pilar. So much work to do on her.

"But (a) Mr. Kim was annoyed or upset, and (b) he freaking disappeared from an office with only one door!"

"Well, I don't know about that. But I don't think it's anything. Mr. Quinn works for the FBI sometimes, and he was a student here too. I don't see how it's any big deal."

"Did I mention the part about Mr. Kim disappearing? From an office with only one door? And the word 'MITHRAS' on the pad of paper and Mrs. Marquardt being all shocked when she saw it? Did I not mention that?"

"I think you've watched too much *X Files* on TV, Raych."

Pilar had taken to calling me Raych lately, short for Rachel. Jamie used to call me that. I have to admit I kind of liked it. If it wasn't for Pilar staring at me all the time and keeping me up all night with the sleep-talking, we could be pals.

"Mr. Kim probably just stepped out when you were down the hall. And Mrs. Marquardt is weird anyway. I think you've let your imagination run away with you."

Sometimes you can't find a sidekick when you need one.

Well, something was strange at Blackthorn, and apparently I'd have to find out what it was on my own. Only, now it was late and I didn't have time to go to Mr. Kim's office to demand an explanation.

"Yeah, maybe you're right," I said. Not! "Let's get to Tae Kwon Do class. Mr. Kim will probably be there tonight anyway. I can ask him then."

But he wasn't at Tae Kwon Do that night. Or the next. Mr. Torres ran both classes. In fact, Mr. Kim didn't show his face around the school at all on the next day. No one really seemed to notice he was gone except me. I wasn't sure why this all bothered me so much. For all I knew, maybe Mr. Kim was taking a vacation. But like I said, from what I'd seen, I didn't think so. Something had seemed strange about this place from the beginning, and the unflappable Mr. Kim gone missing just added to my suspicion.

Later that night, as I lay in bed, unable to sleep, something else that Mr. Kim had said to me jumped into my brain for no apparent reason. It can be crazy having a teenage brain. The afternoon of our fight in the atrium, he'd showed me pictures of Mrs. Clausen's sons, the triplets. He'd said that two of them were in the military and another was a police detective in Miami. So that meant that Mr. Quinn, Agent Tyler, and one of Mrs. Clausen's sons had all gone into some type of law-enforcement work. Then there was Judge Kerrigan. Another graduate of Blackthorn in a law-enforcement related field. That was a pretty high percentage of students.

Pilar was still studying at her desk.

"Pilar?" I said.

"Yeah."

"Can I ask you a personal question?"

"Sure."

"You said you were sent here at the recommendation of a neighbor. Was that neighbor a policeman, by any chance?"

"Wow. As a matter of fact, she was a policewoman. She was a detective with the Detroit Police Department. She went here herself. How did you guess?"

"Oh, I don't know. Lucky guess. I figured cops and judges know about this place, since a lot of the kids are here because of problems with the law. Or else they are unfairly persecuted, like I was." Lucky, my butt. Now my spider-sense was going fullforce. Yet another item to put into the "Things That Are Weird About Blackthorn Academy" column. It was mostly cops and judges and other legal types that sent kids here, and those kids all ended up becoming cops or judges themselves. There must be some subtle kind of brainwashing going on. Something subliminal in the classes or some chemical in the food. Maybe the lights in the building blinked messages into our brains.

I decided to change the subject.

"Have you thought about college at all, Pilar?"

"Well, I'll only be able to go if I can qualify for a scholarship. My aunt left me some money, but not enough for four years."

"Ever thought about what you want to study?"

"I'm thinking criminology. Mr. Quinn's class is so fascinating, and I think it might make a really cool job."

Another aha! Poor Pilar. She was being brainwashed and she didn't even know it. Well, watch out, Blackthorn Academy—Rachel Buchanan is now on the case.

CHAPTER THIRTEEN

I Prove My Point

Two more days went by and there was still no sign of Mr. Kim. But I wasn't sitting idly by. I had been gathering intelligence, and what I learned went far beyond weird and coincidental to totally freaky. At least to me. I started by asking around to other students, and all of the kids who weren't sent here because of "legal troubles," every single one of them had been referred to or learned about Blackthorn from someone who was a cop or judge or social worker or in the military. Of the kids I talked to, fourteen had been sent here like I was—go to the school or go to Juvie. Twenty-one kids were orphans like Pilar. Eighteen had been sent here by their parents for the education. But guess what? All eighteen of those kids had a mother or father who was a policeman or some other type of "authority" figure, and every single one of them had at least one parent who was an alumnus of the school. And in almost every other case, the student was sent here by their probate judge, or by a friend, neighbor, or relative who just happened to be some type of law-enforcement person. And that was just the kids I was able to talk to. There were a few hundred students enrolled here, and I'd talked to only a third of them, if that. That was just too big of a coincidence to ignore.

And that was only the beginning. I asked several more students about the Top Floor. Most of them knew about it, but nobody knew anything specific about what it was. From what I could gather, there were maybe ten students in the whole program. They were all in their last year, basically seniors in high school. They kept to themselves and didn't mix much with the other students, and when they did, they did not discuss Top Floor. Like it was totally off-limits. All I could find out was that some of them occasionally left school for days at a time, allegedly for "off-grounds" study or "seminar work."

I didn't know what to do with this information. I was sure I was on the trail of a conspiracy. A conspiracy of what, I didn't know, but I felt that there was something out there. It may not be as big a conspiracy as UFOs or who shot Kennedy or who invented liquid soap. But it was right up there. I was yearning to burst into Mr. Kim's office and shout "Aha!" Except he wasn't around.

Pilar refused to be dragged into my investigation no matter how hard I tried to convince her. Even Alex and Brent, whom I confided in at dinner on day three of Mr. Kim's disappearance, were nonbelievers. They had known Mr. Kim a lot longer than I had, and their faith in him was unshakable. They felt that if he was gone it must be for a good reason, and when he came back he'd tell us what was going on or he wouldn't if it wasn't any of our business. God, how I hated their confidence.

I was most annoyed at Alex, who took great delight in needling me about all this. After I had said my piece, he started to pick at me.

"Don't you think you're overreacting?" he said, reaching over to take a cookie from my tray.

"Hey," I said. I grabbed for the cookie, but he'd already jammed it into his mouth.

"Don't forget to chew," I said. "And no, I don't think I'm overreacting. I think you are all underreacting."

"Well, I think maybe you haven't adjusted yet. It's no secret you don't like it here, and I think you're just looking for an excuse to shake things up," he said.

"Oh really? May I ask where you get this information?"

"I hear things," he said. He took a quick "look but don't actually look" glance at Pilar when he said it, and her face colored. So the little birdie had been singing.

"Well, maybe you're hearing the wrong things and other people should mind their beeswax about what I think or don't think. Anybody wants to know what I think, I'm happy to tell them." I tried and failed to keep the anger out of my voice.

Alex was sitting next to Pilar, and he nudged her with his shoulder. "Did she just say beeswax?" he said.

"What is your problem?" I asked.

"I don't have a problem, but I think you do. Whatever Mr. Kim is doing is none of your concern, and maybe you should just keep your mouth shut."

"Hey, take it easy, Alex," Brent spoke up. "No need to come down like that."

"Excuse me, Alex, nobody informed me that you'd been elected king. I must have missed that memo," I said, giving Brent a look that said I didn't need him to defend me.

"Make all the cracks you want. Everybody knows you don't like it here, and that's fine. But some of us do like it here, and we don't need you stirring up trouble. For some of us this is the only place we've got. We don't have a rich family in Beverly Hills to fall back on, so maybe you should mind your own 'beeswax' and stop asking so many questions." Luckily for him, when he said beeswax he didn't make that little air quotes sign, or I'd have gone straight for his throat.

"Guys, come on. It's not worth arguing about. Let's just drop it," Pilar said.

"Fine. Consider it dropped." I picked up my tray and stormed off. But not before I picked up my last cookie and jammed it into the pile of mashed potatoes on Alex's tray.

"Very mature," I heard him say on my way out. But I also heard Pilar and Brent laughing.

Later that night, I decided I couldn't take it anymore. After Tae Kwon Do class, Pilar and I were back in our room studying. Pilar could really focus on her books. She had amazing powers of concentration, and she'd sometimes not answer me when I asked her questions or not really pay attention when I talked.

"Pilar, I'm going for a walk."

"Uh-huh," she mumbled. She was studying her Criminology textbook and taking notes on a yellow legal pad.

"I won't be gone long."

"Um-hmm."

"Orlando Bloom is waiting for me in front of the school. We're running away together to Vegas to get married."

"'Kay." She didn't even look up. She was lost in her studies.

I left the room and headed back down the hallway toward Mr. Kim's office.

Most everyone had settled in for the night and I didn't pass anyone on my way. About halfway there, I stopped because I thought I heard someone behind me, but when I looked, no one was there. I turned back and started forward, but I had to stop again, because I felt for sure that someone was watching me. I looked around more carefully, but there was still no one in sight. Then I could have sworn I heard a door click shut. It was so quiet I almost didn't hear it. But there was definitely a noise. I walked back up the hallway and looked at all the doors that I passed. They were all closed. I had goose bumps by then. This whole school just gave me the creeps.

My search didn't turn up anyone, but I still had a feeling I was being watched. Maybe it was Mrs. Marquardt. What would I do if she caught me in Mr. Kim's office? Well, I had come this far. I wasn't going to turn back now. I'd just have to stay alert and be ready with a good story if someone caught me.

When I got to the hallway leading to Mr. Kim's office, I stopped and peered around the corner. I didn't want to barge in on someone like I almost did last time. It was deserted, so I scampered down to his office door and listened. No sounds from his or Mrs. Marquardt's office. I tried the door. As usual, it was unlocked.

From the dim light of the hallway I could see that all of the blinds were closed. I flipped on the light and looked around the office. No Mr. Kim anywhere.

Where to start? The pad of paper was still on his desk. I crossed to it and checked all of the drawers again. Still completely empty. So he hadn't been gone on an emergency trip to Staples.

The only other things in the office were the file cabinets and a bookcase along the wall to the left of the desk. I tried the first drawer on the file cabinet. Strangely, it was locked. That was weird. All the time I'd been at this school, I'd yet to see anyone lock anything, and the only other locked door in the whole school led to the Top Floor. But in Mr. Kim's unlocked office, the filing cabinet was locked.

Well, I guess some things have to be private. Like school records and stuff. Or maybe Mr. Kim kept all of his office supplies locked up in the cabinet. Maybe Mrs. Marquardt was a klepto and he had to keep the pencils from disappearing. That must be it. Maybe there was a key around here somewhere.

I went to the bookcase. It was divided into two sections. The top two shelves on each section had books on them. The bottom two shelves held little mementos and plaques and trophies and stuff. I scanned the books, getting a sense of Mr. Kim's reading tastes. Lots of books on martial arts. *The Art of War. The*

Way of the Samurai. The Bushido. Some books on psychology and child development. Plus *The Great Gatsby. The Grapes of Wrath. The Hunt for Red October.* A criminology textbook. Interesting. Sadly, no book with a title like "Where to Look When I'm Missing" or "Obvious Clue Here!"

I looked at the little statues and plaques. Many were little carvings of martial arts figures. A plaque from a Philadelphia charity. A signed picture of Jackie Chan and Mr. Kim that said "To the Best Martial Artist I Know, Your Friend, Jackie Chan." Jackie Chan! Holy cow! Mr. Kim knew Jackie Chan? The picture was of Jackie and Mr. Kim in their *do baks* in front of a banner that said *"Kick-a-thon for St. Jude's Children's Hospital."* Must have been some fund-raising tournament or something. Jackie Chan. Wow.

The next photo was in a metal frame, and it was pretty small. I had to stoop down to look at it, and I saw it was a picture of Mr. Kim and some other guy that I didn't recognize. Mr. Kim was much younger in the picture, and they both were wearing some kind of uniform. The other guy appeared to be a little older than Mr. Kim. He was very handsome, tall with jet-black hair and blue eyes that you could call steely.

I wanted to get a closer look at Mr. Kim when he was younger, so I reached to pick up the picture frame. But when I grabbed it, it flipped forward and lay facedown on the shelf. I saw it was attached to the shelf with a little hinged spring. Then I heard a little hiss, like steam escaping from a pipe, and then the other section of the bookshelf swung out away from the wall. When it finished moving, and the hissing sound faded and my heart stopped hammering in my chest, I saw that behind the bookcase, just like in the movies or a Batman cartoon, was a stairway leading down into the darkness. I stood at the top of the stairs looking down, wondering what to do. But I'd answered one of my questions. At least now I knew how Mr. Kim had disappeared.

CHAPTER FOURTEEN

Does This Place Have Cable?

Ordinarily, I don't think of myself as the bravest person in the world. I don't like dark places. I don't like scary movies. Weird stuff kind of creeps me out. As I stood there I thought, *Don't do it, Rachel. Don't go down there. Who knows what you will find.* I was giving myself smart advice. I knew what I should do is go back to my room and either forget the whole thing or get Pilar and see if we could sneak over to Brent and Alex's room and get them to come with us. And maybe Mr. Quinn. And Mr. Torres from Tae Kwon Do. And Mr. Elliot from gym. He was tough. Unlike, say, me.

But it was me I was dealing with, so there was no way I was going to forget it. Going to get Pilar would be smart, but I might be seen on the way out or back and then we'd be busted. You never knew where Mrs. Marquardt or one of the other resident faculty members was going to pop up. And if I told Mr. Quinn or somebody, they might not let me go with them and then I'd never know what was going on. That would be worse than any of the other options.

In the few seconds it took me to think all of this, the bookcase/secret passageway solved the problem for me, because the hissing sound started again, and it began to close. I jumped through the doorway and onto the top step of the stairway as the wall closed up behind me—as I said before, despite not exercising before I got to Blackthorn, I was always pretty quick on my feet.

When the wall closed behind me I thought I would freak, because it was pitch black. But right as I was about to scream, lights came on automatically and I swallowed the scream in my throat.

The stairway wasn't like a stairway in an office building or hotel that twisted around and went back and forth. This one went straight down. A long way straight down. All I could think of was a mine shaft or those steps that people have to walk down when a roller coaster breaks at the very top.

Well. What to do. I looked at the walls to either side of me. On my left there was a little red button with a sign above it that said "Exit." That must get me out. And since I'd gone this far. . . .

I started down the steps. After about ten minutes and what must have been the equivalent of ten or twelve flights of stairs, I finally reached the bottom. I found an archway that led through to a short hallway with a gray steel door at the end of it. I walked up to the door and listened. I couldn't hear anything at all except the faint hum of the lights. Now I was a little bit scared. What if there was someone waiting for me on the other side? What if I went through the door and it locked and I couldn't get back out? Maybe I should go back to my room. I looked over my shoulder at the long stairway and decided I didn't really feel like climbing it so soon. So I tried the doorknob. Guess what? It wasn't locked.

When I walked through the door, I knew in an instant that I wasn't in Kansas anymore. It took a while for my mind to comprehend what I was seeing. For a minute I thought I had stepped into the freaking Batcave.

The room was huge. As large as an airplane hangar, maybe bigger. Considering that I had to be at least ten stories underground, if not more, that was amazing in itself. But it was what was in the room that really had me freaked.

On the wall immediately to my left was a bank of computers. To call them state of the art wouldn't even do it, because the monitors and consoles weren't like anything you could buy at Radio Shack. The monitors were built into the wall and all had lithium-liquid silicon screens. I considered myself something of a computer geek, but what I knew about these screens was that there were only supposed to be a couple of prototypes in the world. There were six separate workstations where the keyboards were all set up with the latest in infrared mouse technology and the disk ports were smaller than anything I'd seen, so they must not use CD, MP3, or even digital fiber-optic relays.

I couldn't believe it. Talk about me wanting Internet access in my room. This place practically *was* the Internet.

There was so much to see that I almost didn't know where to look first. Across the aisle from the computer stations were what looked like a bunch of highly sophisticated fax machines. A couple of them had telephones attached to them and little signs that said stuff about satellite uplinks. Next to the aisle with the computers and the fax machines was another aisle with a long counter, that had all kinds of lab equipment on it, like microscopes and centrifuges and other stuff so high tech that I couldn't even imagine what it was for.

On the wall to my right was a very large wooden fixture that held a huge variety of martial arts weapons. Swords, sais, staffs, ninja stars, and a variety of other mysterious things that looked deadly. It looked like a Teenage Mutant Ninja Turtle had exploded on the wall. There was some serious stuff hanging there.

And that was only what I could see from the doorway. I walked farther into the room and tried to take it all in. In the middle of the room there was a large conference table with a four-sided video monitor in the middle. On the far side of the room were several vehicles parked along the wall near what looked like a big garage door. There were a couple of gray sedans. There were also a Ferrari, a Harley-Davidson motorcycle, and a panel van that said "Henderson's Dry Cleaning. We Deliver" on the side of it.

Mr. Kim had his very own secret hideout! What the heck was going on here? Who was this guy and what was he doing with all this stuff underneath a school for kids? There didn't seem to be any cameras or hidden microphones or anything, so it didn't look like this was a way of spying on the students. Or was it? Could this be how Mr. Kim always seemed to know what was going on? I walked all around the room looking at everything, up and down each aisle and in each cubicle and nook and cranny, and I didn't see any closed-circuit camera monitors. I'd never noticed any cameras around the school either, come to think of it.

Also, this place had an "official" feel to it, almost like it was set up for a specific purpose that had only a little to do with the school and a lot to do with something else. Time to intensify my search. Whatever this place was, it was no ordinary boarding school. It was a setup or a front for something. I didn't know what yet, but I was sure I was right.

I went back to the computers and sat down at one that had the desktop page showing. It wasn't password locked, probably because no one expected anyone else to use it. Mr. Chapman would have freaked at the thought. I clicked on Internet Explorer and got into a search engine. I typed in "Mr. Jonathon Kim" and "Blackthorn Academy." I got one match, and it was for the school's website. A great place to learn and grow and blah, blah, blah.

I typed in just "Jonathon Kim" and got fourteen matches. One was the school's website again, and none of the others were the Mr. Kim I was looking for.

I typed in "Book of Seraphim" and got a bunch of listings, but the one that caught my eye was an AP story that said:

"Valuable Book Stolen from Washington D.C. Gallery." Holy guacamole! Apparently the night after we'd visited the gallery, it had been broken into by someone sophisticated enough to bypass the alarms and steal the book. The story said it was the only item taken, probably because it was the most valuable. The police had no leads yet. Okay, *this* was news. Wow. Shows you the total news-blackout state here at Blackthorn Academy.

Things were starting to come together. The FBI agents must have come to see Mr. Kim because we had been at the gallery the day before a priceless artifact was stolen. That's why I'd heard the one agent say the word "Seraphim." Did they think someone from the school had something to do with it? All I knew was *I* didn't do it, although I'm sure Judge Kerrigan would pin it on me if she could. It didn't seem likely that anyone here had anything to do with the theft. Maybe the FBI was just being thorough and wanted to know if the students had noticed anybody casing the joint. That must be it. Sure.

Then I typed in "Mithras," and I have to say that I got more than I bargained for. There were about thirty sites devoted to Mithras. I clicked one of them and read through some of the postings, giving myself a quick education. The upshot of what I learned was that Mithras is an ancient god, prominent in several Middle Eastern cultures. In most religions he was considered to be a God of Darkness and the Afterlife. Mithras was banished to the underworld for sacrificing a bull, which was the symbol of life. He frequently returned to try to take over the world, and he was said to be able to change from bull to human form at will. Hey! Just like the guy in the weird dream I had. What a coincidence. Of all the freaky things for my subconscious mind to come up with. And again, that word "Mithras" started to nag at me. I didn't know jack about ancient mythology, but that word still seemed familiar somehow.

I also read that Mithras became very popular with the soldiers of the Roman army just about the time that the Roman Empire was declining. Many of the soldiers formed their own cults and built temples to Mithras. They had all these weird ceremonies where they purified themselves and made sacrifices, believing that Mithras would make them invincible and restore the empire to its past glory. This spread through the legions of the Roman army very rapidly for a short time, but then the empire fell and the cult sort of died out. Now all that was left were a few temples and some artifacts from archaeological digs in the Middle East.

All of the stuff about being invincible and purifying and sacrifices sure sounded like a guy thing. But what did it have to do with Mr. Kim and why would the FBI be asking him about it? He was a headmaster at a boarding school, not some low-rent James Bond.

Okay. I'm not really as dense as that. Really. Mr. Kim somehow taught all of his students to become cops, judges, or FBI agents. He was a major martial arts butt-kicker. He had a mini-Pentagon underneath his office. So there was clearly more going on with Mr. Kim than him being a simple headmaster at a school for misguided youth. And all that was leaving out the fact that Mr. Kim was also buddies with Jackie Chan. Let's not forget that.

I needed Pilar's powers of concentration to help me muddle through all this. But she would probably have to see it to believe it. My mind was spinning so much that I almost missed the best clue. Down at the bottom of the screen was an e-mail message that had been reduced but not closed. Mr. Kim must have been in a hurry and probably thought he closed it.

Now, I want to go on record here that just because I tend to be a smart aleck sometimes and I have had a few unfortunate misunderstandings with the law, I'm not really a bad person. I know you shouldn't read other people's e-mail. It's probably a felony or something. Unless, of course, it was an emergency and someone's life could be saved by the information in the e-mail, like Mr. Kim's—right?

I clicked on the e-mail and it expanded to fill the screen in front of me. It explained very little, but as I would soon find out, it also explained a lot. The e-mail read:

> *Jonathon,*
> *My old friend. I have the book. Of course you already knew that. I think I'll be putting it to good use. I'd say don't try to find me but I know that you will. Trust me, it will only end badly.*
> *Yours,*
> *Sam Rith*

CHAPTER FIFTEEN

Finally They Believe Me . . . Sort of

Aha! Somebody named Sam had stolen the *Book of Seraphim*! And he somehow knew Mr. Kim. And he wanted to brag about stealing the book. Maybe Mr. Kim had once been a cop and he'd busted this Sam guy, so when Mr. Rith got out of the big house, he wanted to make a big theft and rub Mr. Kim's nose in it. Sort of like how Lex Luthor is always taunting Superman.

So Mr. Kim must have taken off to find this guy and get the book back. Now it all sort of made sense. I looked over to where the cars were parked and noticed there was one missing. Or at least there was a space that could hold a car or truck. So Mr. Kim must have come down here, gotten the e-mail, and taken off after this bad guy Sam. All by himself. With no backup. Had he never seen the *Lethal Weapon* movies? Didn't he know what a bad idea it was to take off after a criminal with no backup?

What was I was going to do with this information? I didn't think it would be a good idea to let any of the teachers know that I'd been snooping around in Mr. Kim's office and had found the Fortress of Solitude. On the other hand, I had to tell someone or I was going to explode.

I looked at my watch. I'd been gone an hour. I needed to find a way to get Pilar down here.

I printed out a copy of the e-mail, then headed back up the stairs to Mr. Kim's office. I was huffing and puffing quite a bit when I got to the top of the stairs, so I paused for a minute, making sure I couldn't hear anyone on the other side. No sounds. I pushed the little red button, and as the bookcase swung out of the wall, I stepped back into Mr. Kim's office.

It took me a few seconds to realize what was wrong. I knew that I had left the light on in Mr. Kim's office—but now the lights were off. I stood there, frozen in the dark, not sure what to do. Maybe someone had just seen the light on and come in to turn it off. Or maybe someone was lurking in the darkness right now, waiting to murder me in some horrible fashion. I was completely freaked out. I had to get out of there.

There was little, if any, light coming in through the blinds, and the office was cloaked in darkness. I started toward the door. Luckily Mr. Kim wasn't big on office furnishings, so I didn't have to worry about tripping over anything. I reached to grab the doorknob, and that was when I felt a hand go over my mouth and an arm come around to pin me from behind. The arms were strong, and they pulled me around so that our backs were to the wall beside the door. I tried to scream and struggle, but I couldn't get any air. I kicked back with my legs and worked one of my arms free and pulled at the hand that covered my mouth.

A voice hissed in my ear. "Quiet. Mrs. Marquardt is in her office with the door open." The voice sounded familiar. I stopped fighting. "I'm going to let go. Be quiet or we'll be caught. Okay?" The arm around me relaxed a little, and I nodded. The hand moved away from my mouth. I sucked in a huge breath of air.

"Who—" I started. But whoever it was shushed me. I could see the dark form move around me and grab the doorknob. The door opened ever so slightly, and when it did a small sliver of light came in and illuminated Brent's face peering into the hall. He closed the door silently.

"Brent, what are you doing here?" I said. My heart rate slowly started returning to normal.

"Shhh. She's still there. I saw you leave the girls' wing and you looked like you were up to something, so I followed you."

"So it was you. I *knew* I heard someone behind me," I said.

"I followed you into Mr. Kim's office, but when I got here you had vanished. Where did you go?"

"I'll explain later. Why'd you turn the lights off?"

"I didn't want to attract attention. I was going to go back to my room, but when I opened the door to check the hallway, I spotted Mrs. Marquardt and had to wait. Then you came out of the wall. What's going on?" He sounded concerned.

Suddenly we heard Mrs. Marquardt's door close. We kept

quiet as her footsteps headed down the hall. When we were sure it was safe, Brent flipped on the light.

"I've got big news. Can you get Alex and meet me in our room in fifteen minutes?" I said.

"No, I don't think so," he said.

"Why not?" I asked.

"It's against the rules," he said.

"Against the rules?"

"Yep."

Getting information out of this guy wasn't easy. I mean, I'd known him only a short time and he always seemed kind of quiet, but come on, talk already.

"What rules?"

"The rules against boys being in the girls' wing," he said.

Oh. Those rules. Hmm. Where could we meet after hours and not be seen?

"Okay, fine. Can you get Alex and meet us in the rec room? In fifteen minutes?" I remembered Pilar saying that hardly anyone used it.

Brent nodded. He opened the door slightly to check the hall. It was clear. We moved out of the office quickly and split up to head off to our rooms.

Pilar was still at her desk with her nose buried in her Criminal Justice text. She wasn't crazy about leaving her books, but she eventually relented and fifteen minutes later we were all in the rec room.

"You are not going to believe what I've just seen," I said.

"It wouldn't by any chance be the answers to Friday's

Cultures quiz, would it?" Pilar said.

"No. Listen, I have to swear you all to secrecy about this. I've done something I probably shouldn't have, but I had a good reason."

Suddenly there was a hint of suspicion in their eyes. I was a little hurt at first, but then I remembered that they were here at Blackthorn on a slightly different agenda from me. The last thing they probably wanted or needed was someone that was going to get them into trouble.

"What is it now?" Alex asked, adding "crackpot" under his breath. I shot him my best hairy eyeball. He was unfazed. *Stay on point, Rachel. Don't let Alex goad you into an argument,* I told myself.

"Something weird *is* going on, and I have proof." I handed Pilar the copy of the e-mail. Alex and Brent read it over her shoulder.

Pilar looked at me, puzzled. "Where did you get this?"

"If I told you that Mr. Kim has an enormous secret hideaway about ten stories below his office, filled with super-computers, martial arts weapons, mad-scientist laboratory equipment, and a bunch of other high-tech gear, would you believe me?"

"Yeah. Right. Seriously, where did you get this?" Alex asked.

"No, it's true," said Brent. "At least some of it. I saw her go into Mr. Kim's office and disappear. She must have gone somewhere," he said. I gave him a grateful look. He shrugged.

"Look, you don't have to believe it until you see it, but listen to this. I found out that the *Book of Seraphim* was stolen.

That must be what the agents were talking to Mr. Kim about. Then some guy named Sam e-mails Mr. Kim that he has the book. And now Mr. Kim has been gone for almost four days. Something is definitely up. What if he's in trouble?"

The thought of Mr. Kim in trouble clearly bothered Pilar. "Why do you say that?" she asked. Her voice was tighter.

"Because he looked very upset in the hallway that morning, and Mr. Kim doesn't get upset. Plus this e-mail says 'old friend' and 'don't come after me because it will end badly.' That's a threat. Somebody would have to be a pretty bad hombre to threaten Mr. Kim like that."

Pilar continued to stare at the e-mail. She was quiet for several minutes. I could tell she was perplexed. Alex was still muttering "nutcase" and "squirrelly" under his breath, but I was doing a good job of ignoring him. So far.

"Didn't you say that you saw the word 'MITHRAS' written on the pad of paper in Mr. Kim's office?" she asked.

"Yes, why?"

"Because this signature, 'Sam Rith,' is an anagram for Mithras."

"A what-o-gram?"

"Anagram."

"Isn't that something someone delivers to your door?"

"No. That's a telegram. An anagram is when you mix up the letters of a word to make a different word. Sam Rith is an anagram of Mithras. What do you suppose that means?" She looked up at me.

"I don't know, but I read some stuff about Mithras on the

Internet. He was this ancient god that was popular with the Roman army right before the end of the Roman Empire. They had all kinds of weird ceremonies and rituals, and it all sounded creepy and totally testosterone-driven."

"Hmm. I wonder what the connection is between the book and Mithras." She said it like it was a math problem she really wanted to study. It infuriated me.

"Pilar, I don't have a clue. But the main thing right now is where is Mr. Kim and what do we do about this?"

"We could tell a teacher or Mrs. Marquardt," Alex said.

"We could. But how can we be sure they don't already know this and aren't doing anything about it?" It occurred to me that if I told someone I'd been prowling around places I shouldn't, I might get thrown out of here just like I wanted. But then that stupid judge would send me straight to Juvie. Aarrrgh.

"We don't, I guess," Pilar said.

"Besides, this place of Mr. Kim's seems very secret, like he doesn't want anyone to know about it. Maybe we need to keep this to ourselves," I said.

Nobody had any other ideas.

"Well, we can't do anything tonight. I'll get out of Kitchen Duty tomorrow afternoon so that I can show you what I found. Then we'll decide what to do. Agreed?"

They were quiet for a minute. Then they all said, "Agreed."

CHAPTER SIXTEEN

We Take Action

Luckily for me, Mrs. Clausen had become quite fond of me in my month in the kitchen. It wasn't difficult to convince her that I wasn't feeling well and might be contagious and shouldn't be handling food in case I started an epidemic in the school. She shooed me off to my room pretty fast.

Instead I headed straight for Mr. Kim's office. I hoped the others didn't have trouble getting there without being seen.

When I got there, they were waiting. Alex had gotten one of his buddies to "manufacture" a paperwork problem at the school's loading dock, so Mrs. Marquardt had gone down to straighten it out. It would keep her out of our way for at least a little while.

I led them over to the bookcase in Mr. Kim's office and

moved the little picture frame forward on its spring. Just like before, the bookcase hissed and then swung out away from the wall. They were speechless.

"Hurry up, because it closes in a few seconds," I said, starting down the stairway. They followed right behind me, too stunned to say anything.

It was another long walk down, but this time I was buoyed by the fact that I had these three with me. Now they would have to come around to my way of thinking. I love it when I'm right. When we got to the bottom of the stairs, I paused for dramatic effect, then swung the door open.

"Feast your eyes on this," I said.

They stopped a few steps inside the doorway, like I had the night before. It was a lot to take in. There were a few mumbled "wows" and a couple of "I don't believe it"s and then just silence.

I led them over to the computer consoles and showed them the e-mail and all the stuff about Mithras that I'd found on the Internet. They didn't know what to say.

"Look, Rachel," Alex finally said, "I guess I owe you an apology. You were right. Something is up. What in the world is this place?" Brent and Pilar nodded along with him.

"It's okay," I said. "What we have to decide is what we're going to do about Mr. Kim."

"Right," said Brent, "any ideas?"

"Well, how far are you all willing to go with this?"

They all glanced at one another. Then Pilar spoke up: "As far as we need to."

"Okay, then. There is something else that bugs me about this whole thing, and that is the Top Floor. Why did Mr. Kim take those agents up there and what is that whole wing of the school for? Everybody has heard of the Top Floor, but nobody knows anything about it. I think we need to check it out."

"We're not allowed in that wing," Brent said. "We could get kicked out of school."

"We could get kicked out right now for being here. But until we know the whole story, we can't decide what to do," I said. "We need to know what they were looking at up there."

"But how do we get in? It's always locked," Alex said. "Someone must have a key. Maybe Mrs. Marquardt. We can search her office. Or maybe we can hang out in the hallway until somebody comes out the door and try to sneak in."

"That could take hours," said Pilar. I nodded.

Brent had moved away from us and was looking at the different weapons and other gadgets that were on the wall. He ran his hands over some of the equipment and picked up a small gunlike thing that had a piece of wire coming out of it.

"I can get us in," he said.

"What? How?" I said.

"This is called a zip gun. It's what cops use to get through locked doors when they don't want to make a lot of noise. You stick this key part in the lock and wires spring out to find the correct tumblers in the locking mechanism. It's silent and works in about three seconds."

"And you know this how?" I was impressed and a little bit

stunned as well, because that was the longest speech I'd ever heard him give.

"I just know, that's all. I've seen them used before."

"Where? Are you sure?" I said.

"In a past life. And yes, it will work," he said. Men. You really have to drag information out of them. But the look on Brent's face said *don't ask me any more questions.*

"Why don't we try it and see? We don't have anything to lose," Pilar said.

"Okay," I said. "Let's meet in the rec room after Tae Kwon Do tonight. We're less likely to be caught, and hopefully there won't be anybody up there."

And that was how we planned our unauthorized entry into the Top Floor wing.

CHAPTER SEVENTEEN

All This but No Jacuzzi?

After Tae Kwon Do, almost nobody ever came out of their rooms at night. The average day at Blackthorn was pretty rigorous, and with studying and all you didn't have a lot of energy left for wandering around. We'd need to be careful, but there was a good chance no one would see us. The four of us cautiously made our way to the back of the school, stopping at each intersection to make sure there was no one around. In a few minutes we were in front of the door that led to Top Floor.

Brent's little unlocking gizmo worked just like he said it would. He stuck the wire probe into the lock and pulled the trigger, and the door opened in about three seconds. We were in.

Inside the door a stairway led up to the top floor of the

school. At the top, Alex volunteered to go in and make sure no one was there. He slowly pushed open the door and then slipped through. The door clicked shut. It was nerve-racking. If anyone came in the door below us, we were toast. Brent went back down the stairs to keep watch while we waited for Alex to come back.

Little beads of sweat started to form on my forehead. When Alex popped back through the door, I jumped because I was so nervous.

"There's no one here. You aren't going to believe this," he said.

None of us were really prepared for what we found through the door.

The entire floor looked like a set for a movie or the backstage of some Hollywood studio lot. Most of the interior walls were missing, and the ceiling was very high. You felt like you were standing in a giant warehouse. Off to our right was a set of rooms that looked like the inside of a house. There was a kitchen, a dining room, and a living room, all completely furnished with couches and chairs and pillows and stuff. Farther down on the right, we came to another area where a bank lobby had been set up. It had a row of teller windows, a safe in the back, desks, and chairs around it that made it look like a real bank.

"What the heck is this place?" Pilar said.

"I have no idea," I said. "It looks like a movie set. Do you think maybe the school uses this space to film TV shows or something?"

"But that doesn't make any sense," Alex said. "If that were

the case, why would it be such a big secret? Why would everybody keep so quiet about it?"

None of us had an answer for that. We found all kinds of similar sets. There was a complete interior of a Starbucks, a 7-Eleven store, and a Gap. It was so real I almost wanted to try on some of the jeans.

Then, over in the far corner of the wing, we spotted what we were looking for: an exact duplicate of the room we'd seen at the gallery on our field trip. There were replicas of the ornate paintings on the wall and all of the display cases with the exhibits, just like I remembered it. In the middle of the room was an exact copy of the pedestal display that had held the *Book of Seraphim*.

"What in the world?" Pilar said.

"This must be why Mr. Kim brought the agents up here. Maybe they wanted to figure out how the book was stolen or something?" I said. My brain was starting to hurt.

"It must be something like that," Alex said. "Mr. Quinn does consulting with the FBI, right? Maybe Mr. Kim consults with them too. Maybe this is some kind of special lab where they try to figure stuff out."

It sounded too weird. There had to be more to it. But that was about the only theory that any of us could come up with. We spent another forty-five minutes combing the entire floor, and pretty soon we were back at the entrance.

"So what do we do now?" Alex said.

"I don't think there is anything we can do, except wait for Mr. Kim to show up," Brent said.

"I *hate* waiting," I said.

None of us had noticed that Pilar was standing off to the side. She had been pretty quiet since we got up here. Now she was staring hard at the floor.

"We can't wait," she said suddenly. "We need to find Mr. Kim."

"What do you mean? Why?" I asked.

"He's walking into a trap. He's out looking for something and he hasn't found it yet, but when he does, it'll be a trap. There is something dark out there that wants him, and it's pulling him in. He knows about the darkness, but he's going anyway, to try to stop it. But it's a trap." Pilar bent over and put her hands on her hips like she was having trouble breathing. Alex went to her and touched her shoulder.

"What the heck are you talking about?" Alex said. "What kind of crazy talk is that?"

"I'm not crazy, Alex," she said. "Sometimes I have a sense about things. I've always been that way, ever since I was little. I can't explain it. Things come to me—ideas, memories, dreams, whatever you want to call them. And this image of Mr. Kim in trouble just came to me."

When she said "dreams," my head snapped up. I remembered my dream the first night in the woods. And then I remembered the word "MITHRAS" on the piece of paper on Mr. Kim's desk. Then that little pulling thread of memory clicked into place. I knew where I had heard that word before. For weeks Pilar had been saying "Mithras" over and over in her sleep! I had thought it was gibberish, but now I realized what she had been saying.

"Pilar, come on. Are you saying you're psychic or something? That's just out there," Alex said.

"What is it with you?" I snapped. "Not comfortable with anything that you can't pick up and break in half? I would believe Pilar is psychic. For your information, I've heard her say 'Mithras' in her sleep several times!"

"You have?" Pilar gave me a shocked expression.

"Now you're both crazy," Alex said. He looked at Brent like he needed moral support, but Brent just shrugged.

"I'm not crazy!" Pilar yelled. "Don't ever say that!"

"You are such a jerk, Alex," I said.

"You're the one running around sticking your nose in places it doesn't belong and stirring up trouble. And *I'm* the jerk?"

"At least your hearing is good," I said. "Ignore him, Pilar. Do you get these feelings all the time?"

"No. Not all the time. It happens especially with some people. Like you, for example. When you got here, you seemed familiar, and sometimes I feel like I know what you're thinking. Not specific stuff, like you're going to wear a red shirt today, just general things. Like I knew you were going to try to leave school that first night." She shrugged.

"You said dreams too. What kind of dreams?" I asked.

"Different kinds. Often I'll see people in a strange place doing something that I don't understand. Last night, I had this really weird dream about Mr. Kim. Only, he was a matador and he was in this large stadium that was very dark and scary, and then a bull charged out of the dark—" I didn't let her finish.

"A bull?"

"Yes, that's what I remember. Why?"

"The symbol of the god Mithras is a bull. A bull that can take human form. And then you have this vision of Mr. Kim as a bullfighter? That's like way too much of a coincidence."

Pilar rubbed her forehead like it hurt. She got a very worried expression on her face.

"That's not the only weird thing," I continued. "I had a dream my first night here, when I fell asleep in the woods. I'm not usually a dreamer. I never remember my dreams, but this time I did. I was being chased by this guy, only sometimes when I looked back it wasn't a guy anymore. He'd turned into a bull."

Pilar looked stricken. "Were you running down a corridor?"

"How did you know?" I felt all the blood in my body drain straight to my toes.

"Because ever since you got here, I've had that exact same dream every night," she said. "I've dreamed about you being chased down a hallway by some weird bull creature."

Alex decided he'd had enough.

"Oh, come on," he snapped. "I don't believe in any of this psychic stuff. There's got to be a logical explanation. It's probably just a coincidence, and an irrelevant one at that. We should forget all of this."

"We can't forget about it, you big creep," I said. "Whether you want to believe it or not, it's all true. Neither Pilar nor I are making this up. How would either of us know about Mithras and the bull? I didn't know anything about it until I looked it up on the Internet. Mithras is an ancient god in bull form, Pilar has been saying his name in her sleep, and it's all connected to Mr. Kim somehow. So why don't you cram your attitude and try to be a little more sensitive to your friends' feelings," I said, pointing at Pilar. Alex looked as if he'd really have liked to shove me out a window if one were handy.

Nobody said anything for a minute. I was thinking about Pilar. I had had a sense that there was something unique about her—the way she sometimes said things like she knew what I was thinking. I don't know if I believed in that psychic stuff or not, but who knows? It would explain a lot about her and the way she acted toward me. I actually started to feel a little sorry for her.

Finally it was Brent, the quiet one, who broke the silence.

"We're not going to solve anything fighting with each other. We need to get out of here and think about what we're going to do," he said. He was quiet, but he was often sensible and right.

"Well, I don't care what Rachel says," Alex said. "We are way out of our league here, and it's all her fault. We should go back to our rooms and forget about this whole thing."

"Alex, come on . . . take it easy," Brent started to say.

I was so angry I wanted to scream. I turned around, slammed through the door, and stormed down the stairs. At the bottom I stopped to make sure there was no one outside. I didn't want my anger at Alex to make me do something stupid. I cracked open the door. No one was there. I headed down the hallway, turned the corner, and ran right into Mr. Quinn. Of all the stupid luck.

He gave me a puzzled look.

"Rachel? What are you doing here?" he said.

"Oh . . . Mr. Quinn, hi! How are you?" I said.

"I'm fine," he said. "What were you doing in that hallway?"

"The hallway? Oh. The hallway. Yes. Well. I was looking for something," I said.

"What were you looking for?" he asked.

Mr. Quinn was still out of sight of the Top Floor door. Which was a good thing, because at that moment the door opened and Pilar, Alex, and Brent stepped out. I ran my hand through my hair and raised my voice.

"What was I looking for, Mr. Quinn? Oh . . . an earring. I think I lost an earring after gym this morning, and I wondered if it might have rolled down the hall here." Pilar, Alex, and Brent all froze, with stricken looks on their faces. I tried to motion them back in the door, but it had shut and locked, and Mr. Quinn might hear it if Brent used his little gadget again. They were trapped in the hallway. And I'd bet Mr. Quinn was headed to Top Floor.

"Did you find it?" he asked.

"What? Oh, no, I didn't. I was going to start searching the hallway back toward the *do jang*. Listen, I hate to ask, but would you mind helping me look? My grandmother bought me these earrings, and I really would like to find it."

"Uh . . . I'm kind of busy, but . . . but, okay, sure, I'll help you look," he said. I led him down the hallway, away from where Brent, Alex, and Pilar waited.

"What does the earring look like?" he asked. I was so nervous I could hardly breathe.

"What ear . . . oh . . . it's a black onyx, round and set in silver." Mr. Quinn was studying his side of the hallway very intently. We were a few feet down the hall now, and I quickly glanced back at the Top Floor hallway. The three of them peered around the corner. Brent made a motion with the zip gun and pointed down, indicating they were heading back to the cave. They quietly crept down the hall in the opposite direction, and in a few seconds they had turned another corner and disappeared. Whew. That was too close.

"I'm afraid I don't see it, Rachel," Mr. Quinn said.

"See what?" I asked.

"Your earring," he said. Darn it! I was so nervous I couldn't keep anything straight. I wasn't cut out for this. I'm a teenager and thus prone to being spacey at the absolute worst time.

"Oh. Yes. Well, you know what? I think now maybe I still had it when I got to my room. I'm going to go back there and look. Thanks for your help." I started down the hall.

"Rachel, wait," Mr. Quinn said.

I stopped. *Uh-oh.*

He walked up to me.

"Why don't you tell me what you're up to?" he said.

"What? What do you mean? I'm not up to anything," I said. If he only knew. *Think, Rachel. Of all the tales you've ever told, this had better be a doozy.*

"Of course you are. You're sweating. You're nervous. And in case you didn't notice, you happen to be wearing both onyx earrings right now." My hand flew to my ear. Sure enough, I was wearing both earrings. How stupid could I be?

"Okay, I guess you caught me." I started laughing, that stupid nervous laugh that I get when I'm scared or in trouble. Mr. Quinn didn't say anything. "If you must know, I was trying to get into the Top Floor wing. I've been asking everyone since I got here what it is and what goes on there, but nobody knows, and the people who do know won't tell me, which isn't fair because you shouldn't keep secrets, at least not from me. So I figured I would have a look for myself, but it's locked and I couldn't get in. Nothing else in this school is locked except the Top Floor wing. It's driving me nuts and so I was trying to get in and then you came along and caught me." I tend to ramble when I'm nervous. I'd also read somewhere that the best lies are the ones that are closest to the truth. So I hoped whoever said that was right. My mouth had gone completely dry.

Mr. Quinn smiled.

"I see. Well, I can appreciate and understand your curiosity. But I'm afraid Top Floor is for seniors only. I'm sure when it's appropriate, Mr. Kim will tell you everything you want to know. But in the meantime, I'd forget about trying to get in there, okay?"

"Yes, sir," I said.

"All right, then. Back to your room. Good night." Mr. Quinn turned around and headed back down to the TF wing. I heard the door open and shut. So Mr. Quinn had a key. That might be useful future information.

Several minutes later I burst through the door into the cave. Brent and Pilar and Alex were pacing back and forth, waiting. They all let out yells when they saw me.

"What happened?" Pilar asked. I told them.

"Whew. You really saved our skins," Alex said.

"I did, didn't I?" I said.

"Don't let it go to your head. It was your idea to go up there in the first place," he said.

Same old Alex. But we needed to get back on track.

"Look, I believe Pilar. Something strange is happening here, and if she says Mr. Kim is in danger, then that is good enough for me. We need some answers," I said.

"Yeah, but where are we going to get them?" Brent asked.

"I'm thinking—Agent Nathan Tyler of the FBI, Blackthorn Academy class of 1990." I pulled his business card out of my pocket and held it up.

"Would he talk to us?" Pilar asked.

"Maybe if we speak to him in person. I'm thinking it's probably not a good idea to call him from here. We don't know if these calls are recorded or what, and then they'll know for sure we've been down here."

"But how are we going to talk to him in person? We're stuck here at the Academy," Brent said.

"Well, it's Friday night. There has just been a major theft of a priceless artifact, and the FBI is investigating it. I've got a feeling that Agent Tyler will be working late. So I say we pay him a visit right now."

"But how would we get there?" Brent asked.

"I think I've got that covered," I said. And one by one they turned to follow my gaze across the giant room to the row of vehicles.

"You're crazy," Alex said. "There is no way we can drive out of here and all the way to Washington."

"Rachel, Alex may be right," Brent said. "Maybe it's not a good idea."

"Look," I said, "you guys are both sixteen. You can drive. It's less than an hour and a half to D.C. from here. We'll get to FBI headquarters and we'll talk to this Agent Tyler. It's not that hard—we just have to do it. Don't worry, I have experience in joy riding."

Pilar spoke up. "But even if we can get there, how are we going to find him? We can't just storm into FBI headquarters and demand to see Agent Tyler. And what if we get stopped along the way?" Ever-sensible Pilar was being somewhat of a wet blanket about this whole thing.

"Okay, I don't have everything thought out yet. But you said yourself that Mr. Kim is on his way to trouble. So unless one of you has a better plan, I think we need to do this. Are you in or out?"

I could tell the boys, especially Alex, were close to dropping out. No way did they want to go down in flames with me. But when I started talking to Pilar like we could do it on our own, their innate macho-ness won out and they were in.

Pilar and I hustled back to our room to get my laptop. I also grabbed an extra battery for it and the cash I had brought with me that I still hadn't spent yet.

When we got back to the cave, Brent and Alex were taking a couple of funky-looking martial arts weapons off the board and loading them into the Henderson's Dry Cleaning van.

While the sharp pointed sticks and wooden clubs made me a little nervous, the choice of the van was a good one. Anyone who saw us would assume a teenage driver was just a delivery boy.

"Did you find the keys?" I asked.

"In the ignition," Brent said.

"Doesn't surprise me. The big secret movie set they keep off-limits, but nothing else is ever locked around here, not even the door to the secret hideout."

They finished loading the stuff and we all climbed into the van. Alex started it up as I found the garage door opener. The door led to a tunnel that wound through the side of the mountain. After about a three-minute drive, we were still in the dark with only our headlights showing us the way. Suddenly we came to a dead end. It looked as if the tunnel had collapsed or something. Alex rolled to a stop. The only way to get out would be to back up the way we had come.

"Now what?" Alex said.

We sat there for a minute, not knowing what to do. We all stared at the wall, and Brent and Alex even got out to poke it, but it was real dirt and very solid.

Suddenly, inspiration. "Try the garage door opener," I said.

Alex pushed the button and, shazaam, the wall started to rise. It *was* fake. Alex pulled through, and when the van was clear, the wall came down again. The "door" had been camouflaged to look like part of the hillside. It had dirt and grass and rocks, and even a little tree stuck to it. Cool.

We were now on a little gravel path that led to a main road up ahead. The only problem was, I had no idea where we were in relation to the school or Washington, D.C.

Luckily it turned out Alex had an amazing sense of direction. He knew somehow that we had come out on the north side of the school property and we needed to head south for D.C. In a couple of turns he had us back on the road that led past the school, and we all waved as we drove by. Soon we were on the freeway and headed to Washington, D.C.

I fished a five-dollar bill out of my pocket and handed it to Brent.

"At the first place you see, stop and get a D.C. map." Then I sat back in the seat, booted up my laptop, and pulled out Agent Tyler's business card. Time to start working on the rest of the plan.

CHAPTER EIGHTEEN

The Rest of the Plan

We parked the van on the street across from the FBI Building. It was getting close to 10 P.M. but many of the office windows were lit up and it looked like there was still a lot of activity going. Apparently crime fighters never sleep. I had finished everything I could on the laptop, but I needed a place to hook up to the Internet. Alex pulled out and cruised around the blocks near the FBI Building. About three blocks over, we spotted an Internet café. Perfect. I ran into the café and was on the net in about five minutes. A few keystrokes later, I hustled back to the van.

"What were you doing?" asked Pilar.

"Just a little insurance to make sure Agent Tyler doesn't try to freeze us out."

We headed back to FBI headquarters, where I jumped out of the van and headed to a bank of pay phones on the corner. I took out Agent Tyler's business card, dialed his extension, and crossed my fingers. I almost squealed out loud when he answered.

"Tyler," he said. His voice was all business.

I tried to disguise my voice, even though I didn't think he'd recognize it from our brief encounter in the hallway. "I know about the stolen book. I have information. Come to the all-night coffee shop on Eleventh and Constitution in twenty minutes." Then I hung up.

I raced back to the van, and we were seated in a booth at the coffee shop in twelve minutes. We all pretended to look at our menus. In a few minutes a government car pulled up in front of the shop and Agent Tyler and two other guys got out. The other two walked around the back, down the alley beside the coffee shop, and Agent Tyler came through the front door. As he was moving through the restaurant, I got up with my back to him and moved to an empty booth near the end. He strolled by each table, scanning the faces of the patrons. He walked right past Alex, Brent, and Pilar, and was about to pass me by when a spark of recognition entered his eye.

"I know you," he said. He didn't look especially happy about that fact.

I nodded. "Rachel's my name, covert operations are my game." I decided to see if I could disarm him with my cleverness and wit.

"Are you the one that called me?" He got a really stern look on his face.

"Yep."

He let out an exasperated sigh and said a bunch of stuff into his handheld radio. I wasn't sure, but it looked like his face was taking on a slight purplish tint. He turned back to me.

"I don't know what you're trying to pull here, but I do know that you aren't supposed to be off school property unless your headmaster authorizes it. So however you got here, you better haul butt back to school and hope I don't turn you in."

"You won't," I said, sounding as sure of myself as I could. I think I managed to pull it off.

"Why won't I?"

"Two reasons. One, I know you went to Blackthorn too." His eyes widened, but only for a moment.

"So?" he said. "A lot of people went to Blackthorn."

I interrupted him.

"Yes, I saw the picture of you in your cute little basketball uniform. Wore those shorts pretty short back then, didn't they? And that poofy hair. Totally eighties. I don't think you'd want copies of that picture sent to all of your coworkers, would you?"

"Okay, we're done." He started to turn toward the door. "I'm calling the Academy to have you picked up."

"I said two reasons, that's only one."

He stopped and turned.

"For crying out loud, kid, I'm busy! Tell me the second reason, quick, before I have you hauled out of here."

"I know everything."

That stopped him for a couple of seconds.

"Everything about what?"

"Agent Tyler. Let's cut the nonsense. I know about the stolen book. I know Mr. Kim is trying to find it and may be in trouble. I know that you spent the whole day at Blackthorn in the Top Floor wing with Mr. Kim and that there is a perfect replica of the Gallery there. What were you doing? Restaging the crime or something?"

"Never you mind what we were doing. What year are you? You're not Top Floor, are you?"

"You know as well as I do that membership in Top Floor is classified," I said. Actually I had no idea if it was classified or not. I didn't know much at all really, but I sure didn't want Agent Tyler to know that I didn't know what he thought I knew, which I really didn't. I think.

"Well, I know that you are not involved in this. And you know you could be thrown out of the school for being off grounds unsupervised."

"Where is Mr. Kim?" I said.

"I have no idea where Mr. Kim is," he said.

"Are you looking for him?"

"No, why would I be looking for him? I've got my hands full trying to find a stolen artifact that belongs to another country. I don't have time to look for Mr. Kim," he said.

"Did you know that he has been gone from the school for several days?"

"He's a grown man. He can take care of himself. Now, you get back to school. I have work to do," he said. He turned and started back down the aisle that led to the door.

"Who is Mithras?" I said. He stopped dead in his tracks. His body tensed and he stormed back to me, and this time he put his face right in mine, giving me the cop look. Out of the corner of my eye I saw Brent and Alex stand up like they were going to come and grab him, but I signaled them to stay back.

"How do you know about Mithras?" he asked.

"Why? Who is Mithras?"

"Listen. This is none of your business. You're a high school student. You turn around and get your fanny back to that school, or so help me I will arrest you."

"Might want to check your e-mail first," I said.

"What?"

"Got a PDA or a Blackberry?" I asked.

"Yeah," he said.

"Better check your e-mail before you arrest me."

He pulled his Blackberry out of his belt clip and started punching buttons.

He read the e-mail that I had sent him. His face got a little red, although he was trying hard not to show it.

"What is this?" he said.

"It's a copy of an e-mail. I've set it up to be sent out to a forwarding service. In about two hours it's going to go out to about a hundred newspapers and TV stations all across the country, and it's going to tell the story of how there's this boarding school that has all these strange things going on. Maybe even putting its students in danger. Film at eleven. The press will eat it up."

He snapped the cover over his Blackberry.

"Nice try. But you know what, go ahead and send the

e-mail. As far as I'm concerned, whatever goes on at the school is your and Mr. Kim's problem. I don't know what you think you're doing, but if you contact me again, or interfere in another FBI investigation, I will arrest you and make your life miserable. Am I clear?"

He didn't wait for me to answer. He stormed out of the diner, got into the government car, and was gone.

Pilar, Alex, and Brent joined me in the booth.

"What did he say?" Alex asked.

"That he has very strong feelings for me," I said.

"Funny. What did he say?"

I filled them in. When I told them about the e-mail, they all got very angry with me. Alex went off on me again.

"What is wrong with you? Do you realize what that could do to the school if it got out? Why do you hate Blackthorn so much?"

"I don't hate it," I said. Well, yes I did, but that was beside the point. "I wasn't really going to send the e-mail. I'm not totally stupid; I just needed some kind of leverage." I was trying to be angry back, but I had a feeling that he was right to be mad at me and I felt bad about it. I couldn't even muster a snappy comeback. "Besides, it's over now, so just lay off."

"Yeah, well, what if that thing got sent out by accident? Do you ever think of anybody else before you do something stupid? Maybe you don't belong at Blackthorn, but for the rest of us it's the only place we have. You must be the most selfish person I've ever met. You need to use your brain before you use your mouth sometimes." He got up and stormed out of the diner.

I looked at Pilar and shrugged.

"What do you see in that guy?" I asked. She got kind of embarrassed and looked down at the table, her cheeks starting to color.

"He's not such a bad guy," Brent said. "He can be a bit of a hothead sometimes, but he loves the school and Mr. Kim is very important to him. To all of us. He's just worried."

"Yeah, well, he's still acting like a jerk," I said. Still, I didn't say it with a lot of emphasis, because part of me thought Alex might have a point.

We all got up and left the diner. I was out of ideas. We still didn't know where Mr. Kim was or what was going on. I had thought I could bluff Agent Tyler and get him to tell us, but it didn't work. All we could do now was go back to the school and wait. I hate waiting.

We were almost to the van when a rather tall man in a trench coat stepped out of a doorway. I immediately thought he looked familiar.

"Excuse me. Are you Rachel Buchanan?" he said.

We all stopped, and then I recognized him as the man from the picture in Mr. Kim's office. He was a little older now than in the picture, but clearly it was him.

"Who wants to know?" I asked.

"My name is Simon Blankenship. I'm a former colleague of Jonathon's—we were in the Special Forces together. I've been retired for some time, but when the book was stolen he called me and asked me to help. But I haven't been able to reach Jonathon for days now. Did you speak to Agent Tyler?"

For a moment I didn't know what to think. I didn't know who this guy was, except that he was definitely in the picture in Mr. Kim's office. He seemed very competent and he stood and acted like a military person. He was handsome for an old guy, and he had a deep, rich voice that was full of confidence. If Mr. Kim had a picture of him in his office, then they must be good friends. Heck, the only other picture in there had been of him and Jackie Chan, so this Blankenship guy must be pretty special.

Then, I remembered we had a budding psychic in our group. I looked at Pilar and tried to see how she was reacting to this guy. Maybe she'd be able to warn me if anything was weird. But she just gave me a blank look. No help there. I decided to plunge ahead.

"Yeah, we just spoke to Agent Tyler. It was a very short conversation, which mainly consisted of him telling us to butt out and go back to school," I said.

Blankenship laughed. "That's Nathan, all right. He's more worried about Johnny than he lets on. This is dangerous work. I myself am very concerned." Blankenship got an anxious look on his face. He ran his hands over his silver-flecked hair and sighed. "You haven't heard from Johnny recently, have you?" he asked.

"No," I said.

"I wonder where he could be. Listen, I know I have no right to ask, but the FBI won't listen to me, either, and I need your help. The last I heard from Johnny, he was at the docks on the river. He thinks the people who stole the book will try to smuggle it out on a boat to avoid the airports. I'm wondering if you'll head there with me and help me look for him. He could be in trouble." I could tell he was very upset. This was exactly the kind of lead we needed.

I looked at the group. They all nodded.

"Of course we'll help. What do we do?" I asked.

"Let's take your van and head to the docks. Tyler said his agents searched there earlier and didn't find anything, but maybe they missed something. It's all we have to go on at this point."

We all climbed into the van. Blankenship drove since he knew the way, and I sat in the front passenger seat, with Pilar and the boys in the back. I took the opportunity to drill him with questions.

"So you and Mr. Kim were in the Special Forces together?" I asked.

"Yes. Johnny and I were both military men. Johnny was Air Force and I was Army. We were in a special top-secret group run through the State Department, called the Blackthorn Squad. We extracted defectors and did other deep-cover missions in foreign countries. Johnny is a brave fellow. Quite a brave fellow indeed. I hope nothing untoward has happened to him." He spoke with a mixture of admiration and concern. Mr. Kim clearly meant a great deal to him. I couldn't imagine ever calling Mr. Kim "Johnny," but Blankenship did it with obvious affection.

The fact that Mr. Kim was a former Special Forces soldier explained a lot. That must be why he had the little hideout below the school. He probably still did some special assignments for the government from time to time. Either that or he was living out his Batman fantasy.

"Who or what is Mithras?" I asked.

Blankenship's head snapped around. For a moment, only a moment, his face took on a strange expression and he squeezed the steering wheel so hard his knuckles turned white. That look was on his face for only a second before he recovered and tried to give me a reassuring smile. But I saw it. It gave me the willies.

"What do you know about Mithras?" His voice was a little tight.

"Only that Mr. Kim got this e-mail from somebody who called himself Sam Rith. Which is a telegram for Mithras," I said.

"Anagram," Pilar corrected me from the backseat.

"Right." I was never going to get that.

"He said he had the stolen book and for Mr. Kim not to come looking for him, and when I asked Agent Tyler about Mithras he got really mad. So somehow it's connected, but all I know is that Mithras was an ancient Roman god of the underworld or something."

"I see," Blankenship said. "It sounds like you know quite a lot indeed. Johnny must be very proud of how smart you are. Mithras. Now, there is a name I haven't heard in a while. Not in a long while." He didn't say anything for a few moments. It was almost like he was summoning up the courage to tell us something that was really painful.

As we drove he told us this story:

"Johnny and I were on a special assignment deep under-cover in the territory that is now Kuzbekistan. We were camped in the desert, and one night while I patrolled the perimeter of our camp, I fell through the desert floor into an underground cavern. Busted up my knee a little bit, but I wasn't seriously injured. It turned out I'd fallen into an ancient temple built by the Roman Legions to honor Mithras."

"How did you know that?" I asked.

"Well, I didn't, at first. Jonathon heard me calling and rap-pelled down into the cave, and we explored. There was a lot of stuff in there: statues, gold coins, and on a beautiful altar made of gold, there was the *Book of Seraphim*. I'm the one that found it, you see."

"You found it? That's amazing!" It was amazing.

"Yep. Johnny and I learned that there are believed to be seven other sacred temples of Mithras. A couple of them have already been found. Each one holds an artifact that the Emperor Flavius hid when the Roman Empire fell. Flavius sent his troops around the world, each with a different item. He told them to build a hidden temple at each location, and that one day Mithras will rise to reclaim the seven artifacts and rule the world.

"We told the Kuzbekistanis where the temple was, and they took the book and put it in their museum. It's been there ever since, until this tour. From what I hear, they haven't completely translated it yet. There's stuff in that book even the sharpest minds don't understand completely.

"It's funny: I had a sense about that book from the very

beginning. I knew we'd discovered something priceless and powerful. I tried to warn Johnny not to give it to the Kuzbekistanis, but he insisted. Now it's all gone wrong, and I hope it hasn't gotten him hurt or worse. I couldn't stand that." His voice quavered as he spoke, and I felt sorry for him. He was really worried about Mr. Kim.

"So the very first time the book leaves Kuzbekistan it gets stolen?" Alex asked.

"Yep. Johnny tried to warn their government that it would be hard to protect such a priceless thing as it traveled. But they were offered a huge amount of money by all these galleries and museums, and being a poor country, they couldn't turn it down. So now Johnny and I have got to get it back."

"But how? I mean, who took it?" I asked.

"Mithras," he said.

"What?"

"Oh, no, lassie, not an ancient Roman god come to life, unless you believe that sort of thing. This Mithras is flesh and blood. See, there is a man out there who thinks he's Mithras reborn. He's been stealing Mithrian artifacts for years now, ever since that book was found. A gold medallion from a museum in Greece. Some other things. But the book will be his prize possession. That will get him started on his final ascension," he said.

"Final ascension?" I said.

"Yes. Once it's been completely translated, the book will reveal the locations of the other temples. And then he'll have all the artifacts, and according to the book, Mithras will rise and rule the world."

"That's crazy. Who would believe that stuff?" Alex said. Obviously Alex had large amounts of attitude where dreams, psychic ability, and mysticism were concerned.

"Well, people believe all sorts of things, son. Ghosts and goblins and UFOs and all manner of things. Mithras is just another example."

I suppose he was right about that. I mean, people do believe some pretty weird stuff. So if a guy wanted to run around thinking he was a bull, who was I to argue?

We had reached the port. It was a small harbor as harbors go, in an industrial section of D.C. The ships weren't small, but they weren't the giant freighters that you'd see in a deeper port, either.

There was a large parking lot next to the harbor. At this time of night it was mostly deserted, with only a few cars parked here and there. Blankenship parked the van and we all got out.

"I think we need to search these ships," he said, and pointed down to the dock where the ships were berthed. "Time is of the essence, so I suggest we split up. Miss Buchanan and I will start on that ship, the *R.A. Smith,* and the three of you start on the other end at the *B.T. Franklin.* There are four ships altogether, so we'll search each one and work our way back to the middle. Sound good?"

We all agreed that it was the best plan—he sounded so authoritative. Our ship was closest. I headed up the gangway with Blankenship right behind me. As we reached the deck, I looked back at Pilar, Alex, and Brent and waved. They waved back and headed off down the dock to their ship.

Blankenship directed me toward the rear of the ship.

"Let's start at the stern and work our way forward," he said. I never got that stern, port, starboard stuff, but I assumed he meant back to front. Why did ship people have to have a different name for everything?

We walked down a couple of levels and then out onto a long hallway that seemed to run the length of the entire ship. All of a sudden I had an eerie feeling that I had seen this hallway somewhere before, like in a dream.

I stopped when I realized that Blankenship wasn't following me. He was standing by the stairs we had descended, watching me. I noticed I was now opposite a doorway that led into a large room full of crates and boxes. On the far wall was a painting of the silhouette of a bull's head.

Something was wrong. I looked back at Blankenship again and saw that he had unbuttoned his trench coat to reveal a black shirt and a large gold medallion around his neck. The medallion had a carving of a bull's head on it—the same design that was painted on the wall in the room before me. I nearly fainted. I had seen that same image in my dream.

"Well, that was easy," he said. The way he said it made my stomach lurch. His voice was dripping with sarcasm, and it had turned cold and evil.

"What are you doing? Who are you? Where is Mr. Kim?" I tried, and failed, to keep the fear out of my voice.

"I've already told you. My name is Simon Blankenship. But you may call me Mithras."

CHAPTER NINETEEN

And That's No Bull

"I don't understand. What are you doing? What is going on here?" I stormed down the hallway and tried to elbow my way past him. He grabbed me by the shoulders and pushed me so I staggered a few steps back down the hall.

"You're not going anywhere, Miss Buchanan."

"Who are you?" I asked again. I was scared, but I was also starting to get angry. Two strange men came down the steps behind Blankenship. He ordered them to go out and gather up "the others." They turned and left. Blankenship started walking toward me down the hall.

I backed up because he had a look in his eyes that was completely evil. He was staring at me with total concentration. I had had about enough of everybody staring at me like I was some kind of freak: Judge Kerrigan, Pilar, Mr. Kim peering around corners at me all the time, and now this whack job.

"Don't you know it's rude to stare?" I said. I know, it was lame, but I was under a little pressure and it was the best I could come up with. If I got out of this, I swore, I would write down a list of good comebacks and memorize it.

He didn't say anything. Now we had reached the doorway that led into the bull room. I didn't want to go in there, but he shoved me through the door and stepped in after me. The room was pretty large; it looked like the ship had been rebuilt somehow so that the cargo hold could be converted into this big room.

Blankenship still didn't say anything. He just kind of strolled around like he was thinking something through.

"Where is Mr. Kim?" I said.

"I have no idea where your precious Mr. Kim is. Off on a fool's errand somewhere, I'd expect. He always was thick." Blankenship snorted when he said it, as if Mr. Kim was barely worth thinking about.

"I thought you were his friend." This guy had to be a total psychopath. When he'd talked about Mr. Kim before, I'd have sworn he was ready to cry at the thought of Mr. Kim in danger. Now he only sounded hateful.

"Maybe. Once. But Johnny and I haven't seen eye to eye in quite some time. Ever since I fell into that temple, in fact."

"So that was all true?"

"Oh yes. All of what I told you is true—except the parts that were not. I really did discover the temple and it really did hold the *Book of Seraphim*. A fantastic discovery, and one that I was destined to make. But Johnny has so little vision. He didn't understand or appreciate what we'd found. He took the book from me and gave it to the Kuzbekistan government, not realizing that it was *my* destiny to have that book. It is the only way to bring Mithras to light," he said.

Okay. Definitely crazy.

"What do you mean bring Mithras to light?" I asked. I figured I should keep asking questions. If I could stall long enough, maybe Alex and Pilar and Brent could come up with something.

"Emperor Flavius believed himself to be Mithras reborn. But he was wrong. So he hid the book and the Seven Sacred Artifacts. Flavius believed that one day Mithras' true heir would find the book and bring Mithras forth to shine his darkness on the world."

What a lunatic. Not only was he a madman, now he was using bad metaphors. How in the world can you "shine" darkness? Creep. But he was starting to get really worked up with this story, and it was making me a little nervous. More nervous than I was already. Which was very.

"So you think you're the heir to Mithras?" I asked. *Got to keep him talking.* If he was talking he'd be too busy to kill me. I hoped.

"I don't *think* it, lassie. I know it. And Johnny does too. He saw it. But he doesn't understand what he saw. And he's been in my way for the last twenty years. That will all end soon." He walked over to a little pedestal that stood beneath the painted bull's head on the wall. It was some type of altar or something, and there on the pedestal I could see the *Book of Seraphim* lying open, just like it had been displayed in the gallery. Blankenship put out his hands and laid them gently on the book, like he was trying to bring it to life or something. What a weirdo. I had to think of another way to stall him.

But at that moment, Pilar and Brent came stumbling into the room, followed by the two men Blankenship had sent after them. There went that plan.

"Where is the third?" Blankenship yelled at them.

"There were only these two. They were on their way up the gangway when we grabbed them. We couldn't find the other one," said one of the men.

"Idiots. Search the ship. Make sure he hasn't gotten on board. We don't want any loose ends," Blankenship said. He stopped at the doorway, turned to me, and said, "I'll deal with you later." Then he slammed the door and we heard the latch fall into place. We were alone in the room.

"Are you guys all right?" I asked.

"Yeah. What's going on?" Pilar said. "Why is Mr. Blankenship locking us in here?"

"He tricked us. I think he's the one that sent the e-mail. He's definitely wacko—apparently he thinks he is the living reincarnation of Mithras, or will be as soon as he has the *Book of Seraphim* and seven sacred objects or something like that." I made a twirling motion with my finger by my head. "He's nuts. Where's Alex?" I asked.

"We're not sure," Brent said. "We'd started down toward the other ship, but before we got there, Pilar had one of her feelings."

"Then I figured out that the name of this ship, the *R.A. Smith,* is another anagram for Mithras," Pilar said. "That made us suspicious, and we started to think that something might be wrong. We decided we'd come back and check on you. I don't know what happened to Alex."

We tried the door to the hallway, but it was locked tight. We looked around the room. The ceiling was very high, about forty feet above us. There were a couple of hatches in it that must have been used to access the cargo hold. Maybe if we could get up there and get one open, we could crawl out onto the deck and escape.

I was nervous and so I started talking. "What we really need to do is figure a way up to those hatches. Of course, that would involve climbing, and I have to tell you I'm a little sick of all the exercise that I'm getting at this stupid school," I said. It was true. Ever since I'd been at Blackthorn it was like all exercise all the time. Plus, all the climbing—climbing out the school window, climbing the rock wall in Physical Training. Back in Beverly Hills the only climbing I ever did was over Jamie to get to a clearance rack at the Gap.

But while I was in midrant, Pilar and Brent were already taking action. They maneuvered some of the crates and boxes around so that we had a mini-mountain in the middle of the room. And then I realized how well Blackthorn Academy had trained them. They didn't even realize it, but they were in full problem-solving mode. They weren't joking around or complaining like me. They were focused on what they had to do and how to do it with no idle chitchat. How well Mr. Kim had prepared them. Whether it was the academics or the Tae Kwon Do training or whatever, here they were being confronted with a problem and figuring out a way to solve it. I didn't know if that was really cool or totally bizarre. But that school was definitely teaching its students to be thinkers and doers. That was becoming more and more clear.

Almost before I realized it, they had stacked all the crates and boxes in the room into a pyramid right below one of the ceiling hatches. Brent climbed to the top, but couldn't quite reach the latch.

"Pilar, you're going to have to get on my shoulders and see if you can open the latch," he said. Pilar scampered up the pile of crates and was on Brent's shoulders in a matter of seconds. She grabbed hold of the rusty latch and started to twist it. "I don't think I can get it," she said. "It's pretty rusty. See if you can find anything I could use as a lever."

While she kept trying, I scouted around the room. Over in the corner, on top of a crate we hadn't used, I found a small crowbar. I stuck it in my pants pocket and started to crawl up the stack. I was about halfway up when the latch door flew open with a screech of rusted metal and Alex appeared, staring down at us.

"Did you guys order a pizza?" he joked.

Alex reached down and grabbed Pilar by her arms, pulling her up and out.

"Rachel, come on up and I'll boost you out," Brent said.

I was almost to the top when an explosion rocked the ship. The stack of crates that Pilar and Brent had carefully balanced started to tip. It seemed like it happened in slow motion, but I saw Alex reach down through the hatch and grab Brent by the arms. The crate that Brent stood on fell away, and he was dangling in midair. Then I lost sight of him, because another explosion sent shock waves through the room and I was falling through the air to the floor below.

CHAPTER TWENTY

Don't Have a Cow

I came to a few minutes later. I could smell smoke coming from somewhere. Alex and Brent were looking down at me from the hatch above and hollering for me to wake up. Miraculously I had landed on some packing material and it had mostly cushioned my fall. None of the crates fell on me either, which was incredibly lucky. I had reinjured my wrist, though, and I was going to have a major headache. Ever since I'd come to this school, I'd had nothing but bumps and bruises. I couldn't wait for spring break. Did Blackthorn even have a spring break? They probably sent everyone out west to climb the Rockies.

"Are you all right?" Brent called down to me.

"Yeah, I think so." I stood up and shook my head. "What's going on? What was that explosion?"

"Something is burning on the back of the ship. Looks like some containers or something exploded. Hang on. Alex went to look for some rope to try to get you out of there," he said.

But I couldn't wait. Smoke was pouring into the room from the open hatch, and the only door out was locked. I started to push one of the big crates back toward the hatch, but I didn't think I'd be able to get them stacked up by myself.

I was thinking that maybe this wasn't going to turn out well, when the door screeched open and Blankenship came in. He paused to glance at the open hatch and the crates that had fallen all over the place. Then he strode over to me and grabbed my arm.

"Let's go," he said.

He started dragging me toward the door. I reached for the little crowbar I had stuck in my pocket, swung it around as hard as I could, and brought it crashing down on his elbow. He screamed in agony and grabbed his left arm. Score one for Rachel Buchanan. I started to run for the door when I heard a whirring sound behind me. Brent hollered for me to look out, and I turned to see Blankenship advancing on me with a whirling nun-chukka in his right hand. It was going around and around faster than I could see. I screamed and ducked as he flicked the weapon toward me and it whizzed right over my head. Blankenship was about to launch another strike when his legs suddenly went out from under him and he landed on his back.

It was Mr. Kim! He had swung down through the hatch on a cable harness attached to his belt, right into Blankenship, sending him sprawling. Mr. Kim disconnected the cable from his belt and stepped between me and Blankenship as Simon scrambled to his feet. He was still clutching his sore arm. I have to admit that made me feel kind of good.

"Enough, Simon! It's over," Mr. Kim shouted.

Simon lunged at Mr. Kim with a roar. At the last second he stopped, pivoted, and launched a spin kick at Mr. Kim's head. Mr. Kim grabbed his foot and kicked him twice in the rib cage. Blankenship went down momentarily but jumped to his feet. He feinted a punch with his good arm and then managed to get off a kick at Mr. Kim's chest. It caught Mr. Kim square and sent him to the ground.

That startled me. I was used to seeing Mr. Kim in practice at the *do jang,* and the thought that he could be taken down by anyone was a shock. But then I remembered that Blankenship was in the Special Forces too, and he probably knew his way around the martial arts just like Mr. Kim. The smoke was getting thicker, stinging my eyes and making it harder to see what was going on. Not to mention that whole death-by-smoke-inhalation thing. I coughed and backed up against the wall to make sure I wasn't in the way.

Mr. Kim got back to his feet and Blankenship came at him again. Faster than I could see it, Mr. Kim launched a back kick that took Blankenship in the jaw. It sounded like it hurt. Blankenship went down, but not all the way down. He landed half in and half out of the doorway. He jumped up, stepped back, and slammed the door shut with his good arm. We heard the latch fall into place. Uh-oh. His footsteps echoed away down the hall.

More and more smoke was pouring into the room from the deck above.

"What's burning?" I asked Mr. Kim

"I needed to create a little diversion. There were some containers of highly flammable magnesium on the back of the deck. But the wind has shifted and this hold is filling with smoke. Let's pile up the crates again—and while we do that, tell me how you got here."

Mr. Kim grabbed a box and moved it back to the spot below the hatch. He gestured for me to do the same. We started to restack the boxes, and while we worked I filled him in. It wasn't easy, because it was getting harder and harder to breathe. But I told Mr. Kim everything about how I'd seen him talking to the FBI agents, and found his secret hideaway—and how it needed an elevator, by the way—and how we got to D.C. and ran into Blankenship and got on the ship and were now fighting for our lives. I figured that Mr. Kim was going to find this out anyway, so I might as well tell him while he was preoccupied with the whole defeating a supervillain and the smoking fire and stuff, so he'd be too busy to yell at me.

"I see," said Mr. Kim when I finished. "Anything else?"

"Nope, that about sums it up," I said.

"All right. Let's get out of here."

He started climbing up the boxes. I was up on the first box when I remembered something.

"Wait!" I said. I jumped down and ran across the room to where the pedestal stood. The book was still lying there. It was big, and it was going to be tough to hold on to. But we needed to get it away from that madman.

Mr. Kim shouted, "Rachel. Leave the book! There's no time!" But I was already there.

When I reached down to pick up the book, the strangest thing happened. I heard this deep and guttural evil laugh echoing through the room. It seemed like the air around me started to glow and the pedestal began to pulsate under my hands. I dropped the book back onto the pedestal. The laughter got louder and louder, and it sounded so horrible that I was frozen with fear. The smoke around me started to thicken, and for a moment I thought I saw a bull standing on human legs in front of me. The bull-man-thing put its head back and roared. It was the most horrible sound I'd ever heard, and it felt like it cut right through me to the center of my soul. The creature looked at me and its eyes turned red. Flames shot out of its mouth and it roared again. It took a step toward me and reached out its arms as if to grab me. I screamed, and all at once the laughter stopped and the creature, if there was a creature, disappeared in a flash of blinding light. I fell to my knees. I couldn't see, and the smoke was getting thicker and I couldn't breathe very well. I struggled up and grabbed the book and stumbled my way back to Mr. Kim.

"Did you see that?" I yelled.

"See what?" said Mr. Kim. He was standing on the pile of boxes, waiting for me.

"That bull-man-thing? Over there, when I went to get the book? Didn't you hear it?"

Mr. Kim looked at me, and his face was stricken. But he tried to hide his reaction.

"I didn't see anything," he said. "Probably the smoke is playing tricks with your eyes. Come on." Smoke playing tricks. Yeah, that must be it. Either that or I've just gone completely insane.

We started our climb toward the hatch, with smoke billowing down around us. Alex and Brent were still waiting for us. We were about halfway up the pile when disaster struck. Another explosion rocked the ship, sending us falling to the floor. More smoke rushed into the hold.

"What do we do now? I can hardly breathe," I said, coughing.

The cable that Mr. Kim had ridden down into the hold was still hanging from the hatch above. He grabbed it and fastened it into a little black gizmo that was attached to his belt.

"I don't know if this will hold both of us, but we have to try," he said.

He locked his arms around my waist and flicked a little switch on the cable thing. There was a whirring noise and we started shooting up the cable to the hatch. I held on to the book with one hand and Mr. Kim with the other. When we got almost to the top, our ascent slowed and it sounded like the motor in the gadget was losing power. I could see Alex and Brent waiting for us, arms outstretched to grab us when we got close enough.

We were almost there when the cable snapped and we started to fall. I screamed and felt myself floating in the air for a second. Then I stopped with a lurch. Alex and Brent had managed to grab Mr. Kim's free hand, and he still held me with his other arm. They pulled us through the hatch and onto the deck.

I lay there, trying to get some fresh air. It was better air than what was in the hold, but it was still smoky. Pilar helped me to my feet.

Off at the end of the ship I could see several containers in flames. It was pretty clear we needed to get off the ship. In the distance I could hear sirens; it sounded like fire trucks were on their way.

We cut across the deck toward the gangway. Suddenly Blankenship and his guards burst out of the smoke in front of us.

"Give me that book," Blankenship snarled.

Mr. Kim moved in front of me.

"We're leaving, Simon. The police and the FBI will be here in moments. It's over," Mr. Kim said.

"Oh, it's not over, Johnny, not by a long shot. That book is mine. Every great religion needs its messiah, and Mithras has called me to be the one. You know it, Johnny. You saw it with your own eyes." His eyes were glazing over. In my head, or maybe it wasn't in my head, I thought I heard that laughter again. I looked around, but nobody else seemed to hear it. *Okay, I guess Rachel is now the mayor of Crazy Town.*

"It's wrong, Simon. You're wrong. All you've done is cause death and sorrow, ever since we found this book," Mr. Kim said.

"Give me that book or you'll die right here," he said.

He reached behind him with his good arm and pulled out a pistol, which he pointed right at Mr. Kim.

"Give me the book, lassie, or he dies." Blankenship's two

guards moved around us, one of them behind Alex and the other behind me to my right.

Alex hissed at me to give him the book. That was when I started laughing again. Yep. That whole nervous-laughter thing, just like in the car that night with Boozer and the others. I was laughing away like a lunatic. It was several seconds before I could pull myself together. Not my fault; I rattle easily.

"What's so funny?" Blankenship said.

"You, bull breath," I said. "You're full of it. You shoot that gun and this book is going right over the side and into the water. I'm done listening to your mystical hoo-hah. I've had enough." That evil laughter I'd heard down in the hold started in my head again, louder than ever. I had to concentrate to force it down so I could continue.

Mr. Kim spoke. "Rachel, calm down. Go ahead and give the book to him." But I shushed him. I was on a roll.

"For the last few months I've had nothing but people telling me what to do. I've been shipped across the country and bossed around and forced to start exercising regularly. I have to work in a kitchen and I'm not allowed to get on the Internet and there's no TV. To top it all off, I've had to listen to your Mithras 'conquer this' and 'invincible that' crapola. I'm done. From now on, Rachel Buchanan is in charge." I took the book in one hand and held it out over the railing of the ship.

"Now, you are going to back up and we're going down that gangway, or I'm going to turn your precious book into a personal flotation device. Got it?"

Blankenship looked at me and laughed. But it was a nervous

laugh. I could tell. He clearly didn't want me handling the book like this.

"Rachel," Mr. Kim said, "the book is not important. I don't want you or my other students to be hurt in any way. Please. Give Simon the book."

"No!" I shouted.

"Don't be ridiculous. Put the book down," Blankenship said. He made a move as if to lunge at me, but I jumped back and held the book farther out over the rail. He screamed at me to stop.

"You stupid girl! That book is priceless. You'll ruin it!"

"Yep. That's the plan." I took a step toward him. "Now, back up or this book sleeps with the fishes! Move it!"

Just then there was a loud hissing sound and one of the containers at the rear of the ship made a loud popping noise as it exploded. It sent a rumble through the ship, and we all fell to the deck. Blankenship tried to scramble to me and grab the book, but with his bad arm, he missed and I seized it back and jumped to my feet. We all stood back up and he pointed the gun at me this time. I was still near the rail of the deck, holding the book over the side.

"Go ahead, shoot me and you lose the book," I said. To be perfectly honest, I was really hoping that he wouldn't shoot me. I was hoping that a lot. But control of the book was the only way out of this alive, as far as I could see.

"Simon, harm one hair on her head and I swear . . . ," Mr. Kim said.

"Shut up, Johnny, you small-minded simpleton!" Blankenship

yelled at Mr. Kim. "Now, give me that book!" He pulled back the hammer on the gun and pointed it straight at me.

"No!" I yelled.

Blankenship screamed a scream of anger and frustration. For a moment I thought he was really going to kill me. I was scared and started to shake with fear. I was afraid I was going to drop the book anyway and then he would shoot me. I could hear the laughter in my head again, louder now, and I saw Blankenship scream and clutch at his head with his damaged arm, while the other arm held tight to the gun. Then Alex saved the day.

"Rachel, *chwa dwi chagi!*" Alex shouted. Without even thinking, I went into a fighting stance and kicked back with my right foot. This was the Tae Kwon Do move where I was supposed to kick with my left foot, but, as Alex knew perfectly well, I still didn't have this technique quite right. My kick connected solidly with the guard sneaking up on my right, and he went down with a thud. Ha!

When I did that, Alex launched a back kick at the other guard that hit him square in the chin, and before anyone could do anything, Mr. Kim dropped to the floor and swept Simon's legs out from under him. Blankenship crashed to the ground.

"Run!" yelled Mr. Kim. We took off, scrambling right over Blankenship and his men as they struggled to get to their feet. I'd almost made it when Simon reached out and grabbed my foot. I tripped and went down hard. The book skittered out of my hand, slid across the deck, and over the side.

I heard it splash into the water. Behind me Blankenship

screamed with anger, and for a moment I could have sworn it was the same violent scream I had heard from the creature in the hold below. But that would be crazy. That thing I'd seen below was just a figment of my imagination. It couldn't have been real. Could it?

He still had hold of my foot, and I kicked back and hit him in the head with my other foot. He yelled and let go of me. I scrambled to my feet. No time to worry about the book now. Time to run. We hit the gangway and raced down as fast as we could. We tore across the dock and up the stairs that led to the parking lot. The first fire trucks and police cars were starting to pull in.

We all ran across the parking lot as fast as we could. I looked back at the *R.A. Smith*. Blankenship and his men were standing at the railing of the ship, apparently having decided not to pursue us. The guy was crazy, but he was smart enough not to press his luck and get caught. Blankenship stared at me from that long distance and then gave me a funny little salute, sort of like something you'd see in a cheap gladiator movie. He put his thumb to his chest with his fingers spread and then shot his arm out straight. Then he was gone. I don't know why, but his little salute gave me the creeps.

We ran to the van.

"You must go," Mr. Kim said. "I will wait for the police and Agent Tyler. But you need to go now. When the FBI show up, the news media will be right behind, and I don't want Blackthorn students drawn into this if we can help it. Hurry."

"But what about the book! We need to try to find it and

get it out of the water!" I said.

"Don't worry about that. We'll take care of it. Listen, your van is equipped with a tracking device. It starts automatically whenever one of the vehicles leaves the school. That's how I was able to find you here." He pulled a small GPS reader out of his pocket. "So head back to the school now, and I'll monitor the progress of the van. You should be fine. Simon is more concerned about escaping to fight another day than he is with trying to catch you. But I need you to hurry."

He was kind of calm about everything. Considering that we'd probably broken every rule in the Academy handbook, he was sounding like the same mellow Mr. Kim of old. Or at least of a few days ago.

We didn't argue with him. We left and drove through the remaining darkness to Blackthorn Academy.

CHAPTER TWENTY-ONE

The Beginning of My Life as I Know It

We were all convinced that we'd be kicked out of Blackthorn Academy. We had broken just about every rule there was. Alex spent a day going through the student handbook to see if he could find a single rule we hadn't broken. So far he hadn't come up with anything.

Those two days after the ship incident were incredibly tense. At first, Alex wouldn't speak to me. He blamed me for the whole mess. Pilar was a nervous wreck, although she made a point of letting me know she didn't blame me. We'd come a long way in a month, and while there were still times when the whole psychic thing made me a little uncomfortable, I thought that if we survived this ordeal, we might actually be good friends. Brent seemed the calmest about the whole thing, but he never said much anyway, so it was hard to tell.

Then, two days later, Mr. Kim invited us down into his Batcave.

He started by pressing a button on the conference table. The video monitor in the center beeped and the face of Agent Tyler filled the screen. He said hello to all of us, then delivered the news that by the time the police and FBI had gotten aboard the ship, there was no sign of Blankenship or his guards. A launch was missing from its mooring on the deck of the *R.A. Smith*. Agent Tyler assumed they had lowered it to the water and gotten away. They could be anywhere by now, but at least they didn't have the book. Mr. Kim thanked Agent Tyler, then pushed another button and the screen went dark.

"Well. What do the four of you have to say for yourselves?" Mr. Kim said.

"I think the question is, what do *you* have to say for yourself?" I said. What did I have to lose, after all? If I was going down, I was going down swinging.

"Excuse me?" he asked.

"Way I see it is, you got a lot of explaining to do, mister. Let's start with Blankenship and this whole *Book of Seraphim* thing. So sing." I was trying to keep him off guard. I figured the only chance I had was to attack and try to turn everything back on him. Maybe I could get out of the trouble I was in if I could keep him talking long enough.

"Fair enough," he said, much to my surprise. And he filled us in.

He and Blankenship really did find the book in Kuzbekistan. They were comrades in the Special Forces, part of an elite group of agents called the Blackthorn Squad. When they found the book, something cracked in Blankenship and he became convinced that he was Mithras reborn.

"Simon was furious with me when I turned the book over to the Kuzbekistan government. He left the squad and vanished. Shortly after that, Mithrian artifacts from museums around the world started to disappear. There was no doubt he was behind those thefts. Simon's been trying to get his hands on the book for years. When the Kuzebkistan government foolishly sent the book on tour, I knew he would make a move for it."

"But why is it so important to him?" I asked.

"Because if its secrets can be understood, it will instruct the heir of Mithras how to recover the sacred artifacts and bring the power of Mithras to life."

"Okay. Ancient book. Crazy guy bent on controlling a supernatural force. That part I understand. But what about this school? The Top Floor? The weird classes? All of that?" I said. "Face it, Mr. Kim, I know this is no ordinary boarding school."

Mr. Kim laughed. "I'm not surprised you figured it out. But I will need you to give me your solemn vow that you will not repeat what I am about to tell you to any of the other students." He looked at all of us, and we nodded our agreement.

"Simon is a dangerous man. Since the book was discovered, he has been building a vast network of followers. He has stolen hundreds of priceless objects, selling them on the black market and amassing an immense fortune. He is now one of the wealthiest and most powerful men in the world. His network spans the globe, is completely dedicated to him, and is full of very dangerous people. If he gets his hands on the remaining artifacts, he could cause chaos throughout the world. I have made it my life's work to stop him.

"I needed my own network in place, both to watch for Mithrians and to prepare for this coming battle. That is the reason for this school. The Top Floor is a special program for the gifted students here. Sometimes special operations need students for surveillance or sting operations, nothing too dangerous. The Top Floor allows them to train here and be available for certain missions. Only a select few are chosen," he said.

"Cool," I said. "That beats regular high school any day."

"Yes. However, as Agent Tyler pointed out, *you* are not currently Top Floor. Rachel, you had no training and no preparation for anything that you did. If the van's tracking device hadn't allowed me to follow it to the ship, it could have been disastrous. I didn't know who I was going to find there, but I can't say I'm surprised it was you. You all could have been killed."

No one said anything for a moment. Then I spoke up.

"Mr. Kim, it's my fault. I was the one who went snooping around and started this whole mess. I begged them to help me, and even when they said not to I kept digging deeper. Please don't punish them. I know you're kicking me out of school, and I'll go back to California and do my time in Juvie. Just please don't punish them too."

Mr. Kim looked serious.

"Will the three of you excuse us, please? I need to talk to Rachel alone."

Alex, Brent, and Pilar looked at each other. Then Alex spoke.

"With all due respect, sir, I'm afraid the answer is no. We're not leaving,"

"I beg your pardon?" Mr. Kim said.

"It's okay, you guys go. This is my deal," I said. "I don't want you guys to get kicked out because of me. I'd have guilt trips for years. Save yourselves!"

"Man, you just never stop talking," Alex said to me. Then he looked at Mr. Kim. "I'm sorry, sir, but the three of us have talked about it. We've agreed. If Rachel is going to be punished, then we all should be punished."

"Is that so?" Mr. Kim said. I couldn't tell if he was upset or pleased with this development. He was a hard one to read, that Mr. Kim.

"Yes, sir. One of the most important things you've taught us comes right out of the Tae Kwon Do student's oath: 'To have honor and faith among friends.' If we let Rachel accept punishment alone and deny our part in what happened, then we have no honor. She was the one that discovered all this stuff, but she didn't force us to go along. For the past couple of days I've tried to blame her for that, but in truth, I can't. We all made our own decisions to follow her. So we can't allow you to punish her alone, sir. It just wouldn't be right."

Mr. Kim stood and turned his back to us for several seconds. Then he turned back to face us. His eyes seemed moist.

"I see. And this is how you feel as well, Pilar? Brent?" Mr. Kim looked at them, and they nodded. "So what do you have to say about this, Rachel?"

"Obviously they've been under a lot of stress and they're not thinking clearly. Maybe there is a gas leak in their rooms or something and they've all gotten light-headed. It's totally my fault. I'm willing to accept the responsibility," I said. Honestly, I couldn't believe it. No one had ever stuck up for me like this before. And I still wasn't even sure that any of these guys liked me in the first place. But maybe they did.

Mr. Kim paced back and forth for a moment.

"Very well. Since you insist on standing together in this, I've decided on your punishment. Tonight in the *do jang*, before class starts, fifty push-ups on your knuckles from each of you."

All of our mouths fell open. "Is that it?" said Alex.

"Would you rather the punishment be more severe?"

"No, sir," they all said at once.

We weren't sure if Mr. Kim was playing a trick on us or not. He smiled at us. "Listen, all of you. Everything is fine. You are not being expelled, and neither is Rachel, I assure you. In fact, there is something I want all of you to hear." He reached into a file folder in front of him and handed me a sheet of paper. It was a memo. About *me*. He read it to the others while I read my copy. It said:

To: Judge Theresa Kerrigan, 23rd District Juvenile Court, Los Angeles, California
From: Jonathon Kim, Blackthorn Academy
Subject: Rachel Buchanan, Case Number 445780

> Rachel has made an excellent adjustment to Blackthorn Academy after a naturally rocky beginning. She has fully embraced the curriculum and her academic work has shown tremendous improvement in the last few weeks. She is bright, extremely articulate, curious, and determined. Her attitude has also improved dramatically from her first few days here.
>
> Overall, I am very pleased with Rachel's progress and foresee no problem with her completing her time at Blackthorn.
>
> Hope you are well,
>
> *Jonathon Kim*

Everyone smiled as he finished reading his copy of the memo out loud and replaced it in the file folder.

"Satisfied?" he said. We all nodded.

"Very well. Now that we've resolved this, I do need to speak to Rachel alone for a few moments." They all looked at me, and I nodded my thanks. For about the millionth time since I'd gotten to Blackthorn, I felt like crying. Only, this time it wasn't because I was mad or upset. It was because for the first time I could ever remember someone had stood up for me and hadn't left me to fend for myself. I had never felt this way before. Maybe that Alex wasn't such a big muscle head after all. I tried to compose myself as they all turned and filed out of the room. When they had gone, Mr. Kim turned to look at me.

"Mr. Kim, you're really not kicking me out? Are you really sending that memo to the judge?"

"I am not kicking you out, and yes, that memo has already been sent to the judge. Yesterday, in fact. That is a copy that will go in your file."

"I don't get it." I was horribly confused.

"Is there something in the report you don't understand?"

"No, that's not it. I don't get the whole thing. All of it. You, Mithras, this room, Simon Blankenship? Do you really believe this Simon guy with his supernatural Mithras coming out of the underworld to rule mankind stuff? That he is the human heir to Mithras?"

"Yes, I do."

Now I was stunned. I had convinced myself that Blankenship was crazy. Delusional. He'd latched on to this old religion and somehow it fed his fantasy of ruling the world. It couldn't be real. It was just the ravings of a madman. Wasn't it? Now Mr. Kim was telling me he believed it was true?

"You can't be serious," I said.

"Don't misunderstand me, Rachel. One's beliefs are relative.

There are many mysteries of the world, many forces and powers that cannot be explained. Do I believe that there is a 'real' god Mithras? I don't know. But Simon Blankenship believes it, and he has convinced untold thousands of others to believe it as well. That belief has caused his followers to do evil. So whether Mithras is real or not is irrelevant. The believers like Simon have made Mithras real and have caused pain, suffering, and death because of it. They must be stopped. Do you understand?"

"I guess," I said, still puzzled. "What happens now?"

"That is up to you. You did a very dangerous thing. You put yourself and your friends' lives in peril, and that is not something to be taken lightly. But your motives were pure. You were reckless and undisciplined, but at the same time you were bold and aggressive. You were, simply put, very impressive. You need more training and more discipline, but I think you have shown some remarkable skills and talents."

"I don't know about all that. I was just following my instincts," I said.

"I know. And your instincts were correct. If I had tracked Simon to the ship without your intervention, I have no doubt he would have made every effort to kill me. I'm sure he had a trap set for me. The four of you jumping into things upset his plans and forced him to improvise." I thought about that.

"There is one thing bothering me, Mr. Kim. How did Blankenship know where to find us? I mean, he sort of came out of nowhere." I said.

"Don't forget Simon's network, Rachel. It is vast. I'm sure he even has contacts inside the FBI. I'm certain he was keeping track of Agent Tyler's movements, and when he discovered your intrusion, perhaps he thought that if he captured the four of you, he could use you to get to me. As you saw, Simon is quite displeased with me." I guess that made sense. Although I wished he had used another word instead of "intrusion." How about "brilliant observation" or "outstanding detective work." Those are much better than "intrusion."

"So where does this leave us?" I asked.

"It must be your decision, Rachel. You know about me. You know about the school. If you stay, the four of you can't say anything about any of this to anyone without my approval. But if you choose to leave, I will understand. I think I can intervene with Judge Kerrigan. You won't have to go to Juvenile Hall. You can return home."

"Well, as I told you before, I still have some conditions," I said.

"Rachel . . . ," he started.

"No. Hear me out. If I stay, I want the four of us to be involved in this. I want to help look for Blankenship. The four of us worked well together, Mr. Kim. If this guy is as bad as you say, then it sounds like you need all the help you can get."

"Rachel, this is not a game. Simon is a very evil man. And you are all in peril now that he knows that you know about him. He will be watching for the four of you. Stay here at the academy. I promise you that I'll do everything I can to answer your questions and help you develop your gifts. But you must decide whether you can trust me or not. I believe with all my heart that you truly belong here. In time, I think you will feel that way as well," he said.

I was beginning to think that Mr. Kim was just as stubborn as me. Time to change tactics.

"Mr. Kim, I'm sorry that I wrecked the *Book of Seraphim*. I know it's priceless and everything. I feel bad that's it's been lost," I said.

Mr. Kim smiled and walked to the wall across the room. There was a safe built into the wall there, with a small screen next to it. He put his palm on the screen and a green light flashed over his hand and the safe clicked open. He reached inside, pulled out the *Book of Seraphim*, and laid it on the table before me.

"But what? I thought . . . " I was stunned. How had he pulled this off?

Then it all became clear. I remembered the replica of the Randall Gallery in the Top Floor wing. Mr. Kim must have replaced the real *Book of Seraphim* with a duplicate. Simon had stolen the wrong book!

"But why?" I said.

"There are many reasons. Foremost is that we cannot risk the book coming into Simon's hands, even for a short time. When the Kuzbekistan government foolishly agreed to put the book on display, I knew Simon would try to steal it. We replaced it with a very good forgery. A trusted contact inside the Kuzbekistani Ministry of Antiquities assisted us in constructing the fake. No one knew about this except for myself, Agent Tyler, and a few Kuzbekistanis that I trust. We know Simon has people inside their government as well as the FBI, so we needed to keep our plan secret. Of course, the duplicate is not an actual translation of the book—we couldn't allow Simon to have an accurate copy.

"We searched the river bottom near the ship and couldn't find the fake book. Apparently Simon was able to retrieve it before he escaped. I am sure he will have a team of experts attempt to restore it, but it will do him no good."

"So what are you going to do with the real book?" I asked.

"We are going to study it and learn all that we can from it. Even if he is able to repair and restore the stolen book, eventually Simon will learn that he has been duped. This will buy us some time. If we can decipher the mysteries of the book, then we can find the artifacts before Simon can and keep them safe."

That Mr. Kim. What a tricky one he was.

"Then I really screwed up by trying to rescue the book, didn't I? If we'd left it there, Simon would have it and your plan would have been perfect." I felt really stupid.

"Actually, no. I think your rescuing the book worked to our advantage. Because you took such great strides to save it, unknowingly and therefore convincingly, Simon will believe, for a while at least, that he has the real thing. Without realizing it, you actually did a very good job." I did?

"So you built that replica gallery to figure out how to switch the books so no one would know." I was starting to see the whole picture now.

"That is correct. That is the exact purpose of the Top Floor wing—for training and practice in various exercises like this. The field trip was a perfect cover for a few of the TF students to install circuit interrupters that would help us bypass the alarms. We were able to get in and replace the book before Simon stole it."

"But I still don't understand. If you knew Simon had stolen a fake book, why were you so upset with Agent Tyler that day? That was what made me so curious in the first place. You never get upset about anything."

Mr. Kim smiled. "I'm afraid I'm only human, Rachel. I was angry with Agent Tyler because his team had managed to lose Simon and his crew after they broke into the gallery. It was our best chance in years to capture Simon, and it was squandered. That upset me. So I took it upon myself to try to find him before he could leave the country."

For a moment I thought about Blankenship and that horrible creature I'd seen in the hold of the ship. Maybe Simon had had help getting away and it wasn't agent Tyler's fault. Maybe he had supernatural help. I shuddered.

"Look, Rachel, there is much I cannot tell you yet. I realize you are not entirely comfortable at Blackthorn. However, I am going to ask you to make a leap of faith and stay. Please trust me when I say it is for your own good." He was so sincere. It was a little unnerving.

I thought for a moment. I thought about my life and how I had always been on my own. How I couldn't trust people and always had to fend for myself. And now here was Mr. Kim saying "trust me" yet again, like that first night in the woods. The difference was that in the short time I'd been there, Mr. Kim and the others had shown me that I *could* trust them. Maybe things really were different here.

"Mr. Kim, I know you mean well. I just . . . well, it's hard for me to trust anyone but myself sometimes. Can't you tell me something about why you think it is so important that I stay? Please?" I didn't know what else to do. Part of me wanted to stay. Part of me wanted to run away and hide and hope that I never saw that man-bull-thing ever again.

Mr. Kim was quiet for a long time, and the look on his face said that he was weighing something very heavily. Then he spoke.

"Rachel, what did you learn about Mithras in your research down here?"

"Just the basic stuff. God of darkness and the afterlife. Worshiped mostly by legions of the Roman Army. Was popular for a while but then died out."

"Did you read anything more about the mythology?"

"No."

Mr. Kim walked over to a file cabinet and pulled out a book.

"There are several variations to the story of Mithras as it spread throughout the world. One version tells us that Mithras was finally banished to the underworld by Etherea, a goddess of Light. Her myth became very popular in the Persian Empire as its influence grew and the Roman Empire's influence declined. In the Persian version of the myth, it was believed that Etherea was sent by the gods to punish Mithras for attempting to rule the world. It is said that one day the gods will grant Mithras his freedom from the underworld and allow him to battle Etherea once again for control of the Darkness and the Light. That is the story, anyway."

"Neat. But what has that got to do with me?" Truth be told, it sounded kind of boring, and I was pretty sure I had seen a story just like this on an episode of *Xena: Warrior Princess.*

"Everything," said Mr. Kim.

He laid the book on the table before me, open to a reproduction of a painting. In the painting a woman floated in the air above the clouds, pointing to a man/bull creature that was disappearing into a cave in the side of a mountain. The man/bull was Mithras and the woman was Etherea, goddess of Light. I know this because I read the caption. I also know this because it looked exactly like the creature thing I'd seen on the ship and that made me want to hurl right there.

But then my breath caught in my throat. Mithras was saluting Etherea as he stepped into the darkness, a funny salute with his fingers spread wide and his thumb touching the center of his chest. The exact same salute that Simon Blankenship had made to *me* as he watched us run away.

"What? Why?" I felt the hair on the back of my neck start to rise and my palms start to sweat. It felt like my body was a coiled spring and if there was one more twist I was going to snap. As if I didn't already have an active enough imagination.

"It has more to do with Simon than it does with you, I think. Simon believes that Mithras will soon rise from the Darkness. He has something up his sleeve. He believes he can summon Mithras soon and start the battle for dominion over mankind. Now, in his insane mind, he believes he has found Etherea. And I think he thinks it is you. So now, Rachel, we have to see this through. There is a madman out there who has you in his sights. And he won't stop hunting until he's found you. That leaves us only one option."

"What's that?" I said.

"We must find him first."